THE
TOWER OF SECRETS

The BEWITCHED Trilogy
Book 1

KELLY ALLEYN

blackbird

First Published in 2024 by Blackbird Digital Books
Blackbird Digital Books
Copyright Kelly Alleyn 2024
ISBN: 9781068650505
The moral right of the author has been asserted

http://blackbird-books.com/

Contents

Prologue	1
1 Anticipation	3
2 A Very Special Guest	13
3 Scorpio	26
4 Jealous guy	34
5 Tricky day at the office	38
6 Into thin air!	44
7 'Let's find you some gauntlets'	49
8 Screechers	53
9 Brief encounter	68
10 Confused	64
11 Zylch	68
12 She's the one	73
13 Tension	79
14 Escape into nature	80
15 Coup de foudre	88
16 Unwelcome news	96
17 The wrong woman	101
18 First date	107
19 Alice on my mind	113
20 Confusion	114
21 Viral spiral	118
22 My family	123
23 The oldest threat in the book	130
24 I'm walking on sunshine	133
25 Seriously strange	138
26 Dinner date	144
27 No two things are different	150
28 No sympathy	158

29 Questions 162

30 Unsettled 166

31 Confiding 171

32 Wrong about Alice 179

33 The bitch is in the building 181

34 Pain and fear 186

35 The plug is pulled 195

36 Ruin 199

37 Crisis of confidence 203

38 Karma? 210

39 Invitation 213

40 The party 219

41 Now it's your turn 231

42 Change 235

43 Touché, Decima 241

44 Shell shocked 243

Dear Reader, A message from Kelly 246

Preview The Witch's Tale 247

Acknowledgements 258

Prologue

You know that feeling when something is about to change in your life? Something your subconscious radar picks up? A mixture of excitement and apprehension. You don't know what it is, but you feel it there, tingling through your veins and hanging heavy on the air.

I couldn't have known what was to come, nor was there anything I could have done to stop it. And if I could have, would I?

Alice Archer
Hawk Bay City

1

Anticipation

Alice

My name is Alice. I am PA to Decima Gauld, the presenter of *The Witch's Hour*. She pretends to be a witch like her predecessor, to fit the title of the show. She seems to think nobody knows, but she doesn't fool anyone, least of all me. Because I actually *am* a witch. The only people who know are my parents. It's not something I make a big deal about, and I only use magic when I need to, which isn't very often.

Today I'm actually going to see actor/singer megastar Scorpio live. I've been his biggest fan since I was a teenager, and this afternoon he's Decima's guest on the programme.

The show goes out at 2.00 pm Monday to Friday. Although Decima doesn't come in until mid-day, I prefer to get to work very early and give myself a few hours to deal with my pile of day-to-day tasks before the action kicks off and Decima goes ballistic.

I had a restless night trying to decide what to wear

and I've spent time on my hair and make-up. Usually I put moisturizer on my face and scrape my hair back in a scrunchie, but today I'm letting it down so it falls over my shoulders and I've put on a little dab of pink lipstick and a tiny bit of blue eyeshadow. I've never been confident about my looks. I think I'm overweight and don't normally like to draw attention to myself. My mother is not one of those women who obsesses over appearance and that's how I grew up. I've never given it any thought until today. I hope I haven't overdone it.

Decima will sneer but I don't care. If Scorpio sees me, I want to look the best I can. I've chosen the pink dress with the V-shaped neckline and flared skirt. I think it's feminine and shows off my curves quite nicely.

The city isn't fully awake when I set off to work at dawn. There's that brief period when the night workers are already home and the day workers haven't yet left, and I have the sidewalks almost to myself. I love this time of day. I go via the main road, though. Walking through the park before it's fully light isn't the best idea.

Being in early gives me time to minimize Decima's reasons to bitch. Not because her bitching really bothers me, but because having a reason to do so gives her pleasure, and I don't really think it's good for her. I rotate her precious Chinese Money plant 45 degrees, then check my sunrise calendar to open the blinds so the sun will shine directly onto her desk when she arrives, but not into her eyes. They manufacture automatic blinds to do that.

If I was still in my beautiful 17th floor office I'd order one for myself.

I scroll through the trail of emails and WhatsApps from Decima. It's the usual stuff. I delete it all.

DO NOT OVERWATER my money plant

Order my Black Ivory coffee – 1 lb. **SEND THE BILL TO ACCOUNTS**

Leave diary **OPEN** on my desk

WHERE is my porcelain mug?

Use mouthwash before coming to my office. Your breath **STINKS** of cheese.

You are **NOT** to chat with other employees. You are here to **WORK**.

Before Lorelei left, I had a really nice office next to hers, with a view down onto the city. Once Decima replaced her, I was relegated to a small stuffy cubicle 18 floors down in the basement, next to the kitchen and the tech crew common room, transmission gallery and edit suite.

The elevator pings. Usually I hear the rap of Decima's stilettos on the tiled floor, but this morning there's silence. Almost. My antenna picks up a soft slithering sound and Decima slides into the doorway in her pure silk, handmade stockings, holding her shoes in her hand and hoping to catch me doing something she can moan about. She stands in the doorway, sniffing the air and waving her hands as if there's a bad smell.

'Good morning, Decima,' I smile brightly, handing her her coffee. 'Are you OK? Are your feet hurting? Can I get you something?'

Darts of malice shoot from her slitty eyes.

'I keep telling you, women your size should wear neutral colors. Those garish clothes do you no favors, and they give me migraines. Come up to my office and stay behind me so I can't see you.'

Today she has a new Hermes Birkin bag, a purple one. She literally goes nowhere without one of these bags from her collection. Nowhere. Ever. And nobody must touch it. She fired a make-up artist on the spot when the poor girl moved the bag while she prepared Decima for a shoot. She makes a point of telling everybody how much they cost. I'm not sure I believe her, because that does sound like a crazy amount to spend on a bag, and she has four of them. You could buy a house instead!

I wait a few seconds for her to take the elevator, then I follow by the **Broomstick** App on my phone. Am I imagining that she's peering into her bag and talking into it?

Up on the 17th floor Decima's office is all stainless steel and glass, clinical and bare of decoration apart from the Chinese Money Plant and a panoramic painting of the city's skyline. She runs her finger down the right-hand side of the painting, which slides silently to the left revealing a doorway. She stalks through and I follow her into what is known as the Passion Pit. The air is warm and silky, heavily scented with MKK. The room is dominated by a thick crimson carpet and a vast circular bed covered in crimson satin sheets, with a mirrored ceiling and surrounded by half a dozen full length cheval mirrors. Steam rises from a sunken bath in one corner. There's a clear space at one end where the camera goes if she's interviewing from her bed. On the wall behind the camera area are erotic photographs that make me flush with embarrassment. An ornate glass-fronted cabinet displays shelves of sex toys, erotic books, chains, whips, clamps and masks. I don't even want to think about what she does with them. To me the whole setup is the very height of bad taste. So tacky.

A door at the far end of the room leads into the studio where she conducts her interviews before inviting her guests to continue the interview on her bed. Often she gets them there as soon as the studio interview is over.

Decima turns to me with a smile, which is always the signal that she's going to be unpleasant.

'So, Alice, I have a treat for you today. Yes! I believe you are a huge fan of Scorpio. As you know, I will be interviewing him very shortly, before bringing him back here to get to know him more 'intimately'. If you know what I mean.'

'I thought you'd like to be in the studio so you can get a real close look before I whisk him away. So get yourself back here at 1.30. Now go away.'

She's been crowing ever since Scorpio agreed to an interview. It's a huge coup for her getting him to appear live. She's built her reputation on throwing curve balls and embarrassing her guests. She gets her researchers to dig up dirt; if there's nothing on the guest they'll go for family and friends. Anything that will make them squirm. Scorpio must be very certain there's nothing she can use against him, but I wouldn't bet on it. She's the mistress of dirty tricks.

I check my make-up before I go back up for the Scorpio interview. When I get there Decima is shrieking out orders and has everybody spinning circles around her. She's hyper-tense, more bad-tempered than normal, although I have to say that she has never looked so stunning. The tiny pink sheath dress is almost transparent, showing every detail of her slender body, including a sparkly heart-shape between her legs. Her 7-inch heels stand beside the sofa, ready for her to put on moments before Scorpio arrives. She can't actually walk in them, but they will set off her long, elegant legs perfectly. She's heavily made up for the camera, of course. The make-up girl has managed to emphasize her long, curved lips which are her best facial feature, while minimizing her beaky nose. Through her black fringe her green eyes glitter with excitement.

I tiptoe over to stand beside the floor manager, a friendly guy with red hair and freckles, whose name I can never quite remember – Spike, something like that. He puts his arm around me and gives me a quick hug.

Decima glances up and says, loudly: 'Goodness me, just look at Alice! She looks a-mazing! Is it a special occasion today, Alice?'

I feel myself turning blotchy with humiliation as everybody on the floor turns to look at me. Sometimes I almost hate her.

The floor manager calls out for quiet and starts counting down.

Decima slips her feet into the shoes and smiles her reptilian smile as the red light turns green. She turns to the camera and gives a little wink, to let her audience know she's going to be having fun.

Scorpio is even more gorgeous in the flesh than he is on film. According to his bio on IMDb he's 34, but he has the body of a 25-year-old. He's well-toned without being over muscled, and his skin is a healthy natural tan. His chest tattoos of flowers and butterflies peep through the rips in his designer T-shirt. He ambles up to Decima, takes her outstretched hand and raises it to his lips. She smiles a lazy, knowing smile and sits down on the sofa, crossing her legs at the knee so her dress rides up to reveal a glimpse of a tiny jeweled thong.

She chats innocently with Scorpio, making sure he's completely at ease. He's relaxed and amusing, talking about his career, and she encourages him, giving little tinkly laughs and occasional theatrical gasps. In fairness, she's a good interviewer, she lets her guests talk without interruption, rather than butting in every few minutes like some hosts.

'Tell me, Scorpio, your biography is out and the reviews are terrific. I'm looking forward to taking *The Real Scorpio* to bed to learn all about you.'

Scorpio smiles deprecatingly, as Decima continues: 'Now, it's described as a 'warts and all' story of your life. I believe there are a few places where you've been very honest about some of the, shall we say, less respectable episodes. Is it true that in the early days there was some petty theft, alcohol, drugs?'

'Yep, that's all true. I did some crazy things and went through some bad patches. I've made no secret of that and I hope that I've made amends to the people I hurt. I think I've reached a stage now where I can look in the mirror and see a decent human being with nothing to hide.'

'Hm. That's very interesting, Scorpio.'

Decima chews her lip for a moment, nodding. Then she looks up and says: 'However, am I correct in thinking that...'

She's about to spring her trap, to publicly humiliate my hero.

I am not going to let that happen. I hurl the **Affliction** spell at her, and a trickle of blood runs from her right nostril, over her lips, dripping down her chin and onto the back of her hand. She stares in astonishment as the drips come faster and splash onto her dress. She tries to hide the blood with her other hand and picks up her glass of water. She takes a gulp, then coughs violently, spewing droplets of blood-stained water over Scorpio.

The screens switch to a pre-prepared film as chaos erupts. Decima is hysterical with rage, rushing around shaking her head and spattering bloody spots all over the set.

Spike grabs me and says: 'Take him down to the kitchen and get him cleaned up.'

Scorpio stands there looking bewildered. With my knees knocking and my stomach fluttering, I go up to him and say, 'Please come with me. I'll wash your T-shirt for you.'

Now I have a huge dilemma. I have to get both of us down to the kitchen in the basement. I can't use the **_Broomstick_** App, and will have to face my worst fear and go in the elevator. Taking a deep breath, trembling from a mixture of terror and excitement, I put my arm around his back – oh my goodness, I cannot believe I am actually TOUCHING Scorpio – and steer him into the elevator. The magic of the moment makes me forget my fear for the few minutes or so it takes to reach the basement. I usher him into the kitchen, sweeping a pile of junk off a chair.

'If you could take off your T-shirt, I'll wash it for you and dry it on the radiator. It won't take long.'

Silently he peels off the blood-spattered T-shirt and hands it to me. I run the cold tap, adding 3% peroxide to

the water – no stronger because it'll dissolve the fabric –
and hold the T-shirt in my hands. Shelley is never going
to believe this!

I am about to submerge it in the water when I feel a
tap on my shoulder.

'You had better check to see if these need washing
too.'

I turn around to see Scorpio holding out his jeans
and stripping off his socks. All he's wearing is a gentle,
amused smile.

2

A very special guest

Decima

When I was first offered this TV presenting gig on *The Witch's Hour*, I turned it down flat. Three reasons:

First, I'm an actor, not some three bit presenter, anchor, chat show host, promotor of over-inflated celeb egos, whatever you want to call it. My job is to shine a light on my beautiful, stunning self, not others.

Second, I am not a – sarcastic finger quotes in the air – *people person* if that's what you want to call it.

So how could I get the best chat out of guests when everybody hates me? Why does everybody hate me, you ask? Well, like I said, I'm an actor and, no matter how strong you are, it's a tough gig. If I don't put myself first nobody else will, that's for sure. Frankly, if more people looked after themselves first, the world wouldn't be in such a mess.

Third, of all the people who hate me, my father is right up there and the feeling is mutual.

So why did I have second thoughts and eventually

agree to the gig? I asked myself the same question. Three reasons:

First, to get one over on my predecessor, Lorelei Thornheart. I never could stand her. Since she left CGO TV she's become an 'overnight success' and now I loathe her even more.

You see, enough folk totally believed she interviewed a real ghost on *The Witch's Hour*. The first ghost chat show guest in history. It all went worldwide viral crazy. The controversy, was it a real ghost or a fake, started a Twitter storm that spread mainstream and has never really died down since.

I'm not sure what went on there, except that after a big row with Dad immediately after the show aired, she stormed off to LA and launched her own witchy YouTube channel. She now has millions of followers on all the platforms, a house with an infinity pool overlooking Malibu beach that she splashes, daily, all over Instagram and it *really* gets my goat. Her cult following has turned into a full-on national obsession. All from talking to a ghost one time. Talk about fake news. Now she teases day in day out with click-bait about her next ghost interview. A superstar musician is all she'll say.

Second, to be frank, the days of in-person auditions, of meeting directors and casting agents face-to-face, or even attending open auditions, are over. Where are the opportunities for seduction? Gone! Gone, gone, gone, with the words 'casting couch' thrown to the dogs.

Recording endless audition tapes at home and getting no replies was getting tedious. Even a No would have been better than the radio silence. The Hollywood No as it's called. So, despite my beauty, my big break was taking longer than I expected and I was getting bored.

Third, he was so desperate, I could name my price. And when I say price, I don't mean dollars.

You see, whoever replaced Lorelei had to be a witch too. Which narrowed the market somewhat. I agreed to be his fake witch only when he agreed to me hiring some hot technicians to work alongside. Hey, work, I said W-O-R-K, OK? Call it Work with Benefits if you like. It panned out pretty well.

Watching Dad squirm, beg and grovel was nothing but a joy. So there was the perfect opportunity to lord it over him. And it turns out that my looks and my cunning get me a long way on the chat show sofa of shame. Viewers, that's you my friend and don't deny it, love nothing more than watching some jumped-up celebrity squirm. With my withering looks, theatrical pauses and, above all, seductive suggestions, I've become quite the TV star I always knew I was destined to become.

I stretch out in the limo, wondering what fun and games my Passion Pit has in store today. I'm tingling all over from my cold shower but that's not the only reason.

You see, we only have Scorpio on the sofa today. He's a famous flirt, but then so am I. There's no way we're not going to get together as soon as the cameras are off.

He'll be singing live for us. Well, for *me* actually. An acoustic version of *Hit Me Up*. All I can think about is how close we'll get after our interview.

Scorpio is a coup, a real local hero who's rarely in town these days. I close my eyes. Oh Scorpio is it really you, sing to me honey, look into my eyes as you lean over to pick up your guitar.

The car swerves. There's a squeal of tires.

'Hey, keep your eyes on the road.'

My driver straightens up, hits the pedal and we're back on track, purring towards CGO TV Tower and my special guest.

My hit rate is high this week. I've shared private hospitality with two out of four guests in as many days, and who better than the biggest star in Hawk Bay City, the hottest man in town, to end the week. The party poopers? Oh, some jumped up cookery writer who wanted to get home to massage his sourdough or something. It's always the cookery writers. And racing drivers for some reason. They only like to tinker with machines I suppose. I'm hard and shiny, but I'm not made of metal.

The cook's snub I took more personally, but I didn't hang around.

My technicians with benefits are always ready and waiting for me down in the basement. My boys are the main reason I finally agreed to take on this gig. When Dad got studio director Josh to put out the word that they were recruiting three new techies, news spread fast. There were queues right around the Tower. I sat in with Josh at the auditions. Auditioning from the other side of the table is more like it. Whilst I was flirting with the new recruits, Josh was flirting with me. He's quite a bit older than me – a contrast to the boys. Who doesn't like to mix it up a bit with their dates?

Some men get turned on by a powerful woman. They were easy enough to spot. Ramon, the runner, is the youngest. A classic looker who knows it with his leather boy style and slick Elvis quiff. Cory, training up to be an exteriors cameraman, is quietly enigmatic with his long black hair and pale brown eyes that melt your soul. Think Keanu Reeves with an English butler accent. I'm not kidding you. Came to the US to be a basketball pro but didn't make it and became a butler instead.

Sean the floor manager is a funky red-headed Irish guy. You wouldn't look twice at him in a beauty pageant, but, believe me, when he starts talking in that accent of his, you are sold. He's got a temper on him which keeps me entertained because he's the sweetest guy you'd ever meet. Is it naughty of me to play them off against each other? Well, I'm the presenter. I'm the boss. As long as they do as I tell them, they'll survive.

I love reminding them that Dad can fire any of them if they don't keep their act together. That would be a shame. They work so well as a team. But they know I mean it. They know I'm mean. It's part of the fun.

Call me too kind, but I'm considering letting my PA Alice watch my Scorpio interview from the studio floor today. She's a massive fan. Who isn't? And she has been working hard lately. I admit she does her job well. Otherwise why would I keep a saddo around whose little cupboard of an office smells of cheese? Literally. Cheese is what turns her on. Pathetic, hey?

She has a poster of Scorpio hidden on the back of her stationery cupboard door. The famous leather trousers promo shot when he switched from singing to acting. Who knows what she gets up to in there. Have I told you about Scorpio's thighs yet? Here I go again, salivating at the mere thought.

We swing over the bridge that leads to the Tower studios and I WhatsApp the coffee cup emoji to Alice. (Whole milk Black Ivory, since you're asking.) The Tower looks awesome today, glistening in the morning sun. It's really called the CGO TV Tower, but everybody in Hawk Bay City calls it the Tower of London, after my Brit dad.

We turn into the entrance and I reach for my bottle of Estephe Gray face spritzer from the new Gold range. ($135.99 to you, freebie for me from the show's sponsors.) Yes, maybe I'll let her watch us from the studio floor. Knowing how much she fancies him will give my performance an extra *frisson*.

'Is our guest here yet?' I ask Reception.

'Yes madam. He's waiting for you.' He bows.

Dad has trained these fake Brits well.

I step into the glass lift that runs up the outside of the building. My first ride of the day but maybe not my last. Smiling at the thought, I whizz up to the 17th floor, looking out at the sea mist hanging low over the city.

There is nothing like the buzz of a TV studio leading up to live transmission. Today it's off the scale. You can hear the crackle in the air.

As I said, I'm not a witch. But this is a secret, OK?

A big secret.

Nobody knows. Apart from Dad and my sister Ornella, his favorite. But he's so removed from life at the Tower and doesn't care about me. Yeah that's right. Did you think that I was a Daddy's Girl who gets anything she asks for?

That couldn't be further from the truth. There's nothing witchy about my unearthly powers. Flirting is the magic mystery game played the world over since forever, and I take my rewards.

We all do it. To make more animals that do it. That's how the world keeps turning. As the song goes, where is the love? Who needs the love when everybody knows that the games of love work better when there's tension, unpredictability, technique, and don't forget the theatricals.. I enjoy being hated. I make a thing of it and look where it's got me. Who needs a long-term relationship? As long as I keep the viewing figures up, along with my hot techies, everybody wins. If I didn't, I could go hang as far as my father is concerned. I'm his tool and he's mine. That's how it works.

My delicate freckled Irish boy Sean greets me, clipboard in hand, ready to fill me in on the transmission order. I take one look at him and laugh.

'So he's arrived, then.'

'He's, er, in the Green Room.' Sean lifts an arm to shield his blushes, revealing a sweat patch on his T-shirt.

I know that look. 'You turned on, Sean?'

He straightens up, lowers his arm and looks me in the eye. 'It's Scorpio, Decima,' he says. 'Given the chance, any man or woman in the world would. They simply would.'

'You mean *you* would.' I give him a long hard stare as Alice puts my coffee cup in my hand. Without a word, he turns and scampers. Alice fusses and hovers around me. What *is* she wearing? I dismiss her with a few sharp put-downs. She doesn't react. She's used to it. All part of getting me bitch-ready for the show. I check the time. Just enough for a make-up refresh. I don't meet guests beforehand. That first interaction with my presence, and the heavy flirtation that follows, is so much more pure and more likely to get the viewers going if it takes place in real time, but I cannot wait to see him.

Sean isn't wrong. I truly *want* this man. Alice has good taste, I'll give her that.

I go through to my bedroom set, known by the crew as my Passion Pit, and get into my daily routine. First, I take my precious antique teddy bear, Digby, from his

Birkin bag and settle him on his special shelf. The make-up girl fixes my lashes on one by one. They are behaving this morning, thank goodness.

'How long will this take?' I ask my reflection. 'Will we race from the sofa to Passion Pit or will I have to tease him? Coax him through? Time will tell. I wink at myself.

Nothing can go wrong. We're playing the same game here. He can get off with any woman he wants, as I can any man. As long as they don't drive stupid cars or write cookbooks.

The show starts off at the formal, old-fashioned, sofa and vintage wallpaper set-up which hasn't changed since Lorelei's time. The famous walls and door that the ghost guest walked through are part of the franchise now. I wasn't allowed to change anything there. To make my mark, I insisted on my Passion Pit, reached through a second fake door. It has really raised the stakes – and the audience figures. My powers of seduction are put to the test every afternoon.

Will the interview stay on the sofa before I get them to my interview bed, or do we make for the Passion Pit straight away and get more comfortable? How long will it take? Who will make the first move through that door? Will I GET them through the door? I copied the interview bed trick from the iconic 70s Brit presenter Paula Yates. Google it.

Could Scorpio be my Michael Hutchence? The love-match of my life? My one and only husband? Never!

Truth be told, my boys give me all that I want, including the odd surprise. Nobody's a better lover than my great polar bear Josh, with the slow smile and twinkly ice-blue eyes; nobody's cuter than my freckled boy Sean with his gift of the gab Irish accent; nobody's as enigmatic as my Brit butler camera fanatic Cory; and as for cover boy Ramon… let's say that he's a man who's one hundred percent at home in his body. His androgynous biker boy meets choirboy beauty and sweet but wicked nature is a turn-on for all of us lucky enough to be on the same earth as he. But then again, could there be another? Scorpio's entitled arrogance as a fifth wheel? Fame is such a turn-on after all.

My show is controversial for an afternoon slot, but I can assure you that it's all innocent fun. We have a broadcast license to keep. I give my guests more than the promise of a lie. That moment of attraction, that's IT. My life. That's living the best life right there. That moment when two humans do a subconscious rain check and go to that different space in their minds. That animal level we all possess or we wouldn't even be here.

I take my seat on Lorelei's sofa and smile into Camera 2.

Sean does his thing.

'QUIET EVERYBODY NOW

READY TO ROLL

COUNTING DOWN 10, 9, 8…'

The red light turns to green and the teleprompter

rolls.

About halfway through my introduction, the atmosphere changes. A collective intake of breath. And suddenly there he is. I glimpse him standing off to my left waiting to come on. Hot doesn't come into it. He *pulses* with pheromones and he knows it. That preening is usually a turn-off, right girls? Unattractive. Emasculating, even. But when a man actually IS a level 11/10, it ups his testosterone vibes big time. Sean is right, he could have any woman, or man, that he wanted.

I speak his name and turn to catch his eye. Why is he deliberately avoiding my eyeline? Looks like he's got his eye on Cameraman 2. Oh Scorpio you player. Such a player. We're both premier league and we're ready to go.

I use every flattery trick in the book for his intro, improvising off-script to show I'm a little flustered. I end by standing up and taking his hand to escort him to his seat. 'Here he is! Hi and welcome SCORPIO.'

His fingers wrap lightly around my own. His touch is both cool and electric. By the time we're sitting down I find it hard to breathe, and, by the big grin on his beautiful face, he knows it. I sit back and take him in with one of my long, thoughtful pauses. I look straight into the camera and draw the viewers into my thoughts. Charisma doesn't begin to explain this man. He's one of those guys who manages to be masculine and feminine at the same time. The famous thighs are present and correct.

'Scorpio is it really you?' I coo.

He's wearing a ragged white torn T-shirt that shows off his chest tattoos: his famous butterflies, hearts, flowers, all so feminine against ripped muscles. A designer original, all of $900 and no change.

'Hey yourself Decima,' he purrs. 'It's my pleasure to be here.'

Smooth.

I shift in my chair.

For a second I lose it. All I can do is give in to the moment, trust that moment, sigh and melt into his eyes.

He opens his legs slightly and leans forward. I get his famous sideways smile and I feel like I'm going to evaporate on the spot. Forget the ghost. What about a presenter dissolving into steam?

'Let's talk about your music,' I say primly, over-emphasizing my English accent to get myself back on track. It's a bit nasty, but I start off with the well-known fact that, whilst *Hit Me Up*, was a worldwide hit, it was a good few years ago now and he's been struggling to match it.

'Tell us about your new album. Do you think it'll get you back with the big hitters?' I pause and add with such heavy sincerity that he must know I'm faking it, 'Where you *absolutely* belong?'

He bigs up his latest single for a while but his mind isn't on it. He keeps glancing off to Cameraman 2.

'Talking of your new single, are you single at the moment, Scorpio?'

'For you? Well what do you think?' he gives me that shy sly smile again. We're back on track for a moment, but then he's looking off camera again.

Then I see why.

Alice is standing behind Sean, moving forward, inch by inch, as if drawn by an unseen magnet. I get that but this is so unprofessional. She's not even standing still, but moving about from foot to foot, sending Scorpio's eyeline all over the place. I want to scream at Sean to get her away but it's too late, I'll have to roll with it.

3

Scorpio

Alice

Like a rabbit transfixed by a striking snake, I stand and gape. He drops his clothes on the floor and walks up to me.

'Come here, gorgeous,' he says, holding out his hand. 'Come and play with Scorpio.'

'But I have to finish washing your T-shirt,' I splutter.

'Don't worry. It'll keep.'

He walks towards me and tries to slip my dress off my shoulders. I pull away, clutching at the fabric and shaking my head, stammering 'Uh, no, please don't do that.' I can feel tears trying to get out of my eyes.

I don't know which is louder, the knock of my knees or the thump of my heart. I'm so scared, alone with my hero, a man worshiped by millions. How many of them would give anything, absolutely anything, to be in my place? But I'm not them.

I've only ever had one boyfriend, Rory, when I was twenty-two. Because of my reputation that I was 'weird' and strange things happened around me, men kept away.

Rory had recently arrived from England and he

hadn't heard the rumors about me when he asked me out. We just kind of fell into a relationship. He didn't know anybody, I didn't have any friends except Shelley, so we were both loners. When I look back, that's all we had in common. We'd been seeing each other casually for a few months when he suggested moving into my apartment. He said there was no sense in him paying to rent lodgings when he could live with me, and just like that I agreed.

I realized it was a mistake very quickly, when he began rearranging all my furniture and reorganizing the food cupboard. All the cans and packets had to be in alphabetical order and according to size. He got quite angry if I put anything back in the wrong place, or with the labels not facing forward.

At first he slept in his own room. We were companions, we weren't in love. It was meant to be a house share and we got on OK as long as everything was done the way Rory wanted it.

It was the second week after he moved in, when I said I was going to bed, that he stood up in front of me and said: 'I'll come with you.' Just like that.

He followed me into my room and watched while I put on my pajamas, then he took off all his clothes and climbed into bed beside me. I didn't know what to expect. He told me to take off my pajamas. He fiddled with my body for a couple of minutes, then climbed on top of me and said: 'Spread your legs open and plug me in.'

The next few minutes were quite unpleasant and

painful. Rory jerked backwards and forwards a few times then grunted, collapsed on top of me and fell asleep.

Next morning at breakfast all he said was: 'You need to tidy yourself up down there,' pointing at my crotch.

I didn't know what he meant, but Shelley explained to me, although she gave me a very funny look. I went to a beautician she recommended and came out in tears from the pain of being waxed 'down there'. After that I used a razor, which was a bit awkward and Rory complained that it was bristly and uncomfortable for him, but I thought if he didn't like it he could stop and I'd be pleased. It was an ordeal that I endured with wretched regularity about two or three times every week. I blocked it out by counting the ceiling boards or writing imaginary shopping lists.

He moved out a couple of months later to live with somebody else. I wished him good luck and gave him a quick peck on the cheek, because we parted amicably. Quite honestly, I was relieved. We were going nowhere once I had refused to suck his toes, which are his least attractive feature.

'Cheers, Alice,' he said. 'Take care.' And that was that. End of.

That was two years ago, and since then, I've left 'down there' alone. I'm not planning to get into a relationship like that again.

'I'm sorry,' I mumble. 'I really, really like you. I think you're so wonderful, but it's just that I can't, you know -

do that sort of thing with you' I say. 'I mean, we don't
even know each other.' I can feel my eyes filling with
tears.

Scorpio tilts his head to one side, pulls a rueful face,
picks up his jeans and pulls them on. 'That's OK, honey'
he says, with a smile.

'I apologize if I've offended you. I didn't mean to.
You know, the thing is that so many ladies expect me to
do that. They send me photos of themselves, items of
underwear, they try to get into my room wherever I'm
staying. You know what? I actually wish they didn't.
Makes me feel like I'm a trophy they're hunting. It's part
of the job, of course, but I am a human being and do have
feelings. They want to be able to crow that they 'had' me.
And sometimes they're scary. It's a real nice change to
meet somebody like you.'

'Thanks,' I say. 'I didn't mean to be rude.'

He pulls me towards him and puts an arm around my
shoulders.

'So come and sit over here and tell me about yourself
while I'm waiting for my driver.'

He steers me to the single comfy chair in the kitchen
and hands me into it. 'Just give me a moment.'

He taps a number on his phone, and says: "Yo,
Mikey. Change of plan. Show went tits up. You saw it?
Yeah, crazy. Listen, bro. Give me 20 minutes - I'm
otherwise engaged with a very beautiful lady.'

My face is burning with embarrassment.

He sticks the phone back in his pocket, and squats down in front of me. 'Come on now. Tell me everything.'

'Honestly, there's nothing to tell. I'm Decima's PA, and I live in an apartment on the east side of town, the other side of the park. My parents live out on the Brent Flats. We're just a normal family.' (I cross my fingers when I say that, because that is SO not true.)

'Lucky lady. Not something everyone can say. Mine was not so good, my folks were always too busy fighting each other and didn't have much time for me, so I entertained myself, got in with a bad bunch.'

He stands up and walks behind me, puts his arms around my neck and rests his chin on my head.

He sighs. 'Yep, all the stupid stuff I did, I guess that was trying to get their attention. Didn't work though.'

As he tells me of his childhood I almost want to cry.

'That makes me so sad,' I say.

'It was a long time ago, water under the bridge, so no need to be sad. Did you ever hear about the frog that walked into a bank?'

'No, what happened?'

He starts telling me jokes that have me holding my belly, aching with laughter, tears streaming down my face.

'That's better,' he says.

'Alice, I think you're quite lovely. It's been so good to chill and chat. Doesn't happen very often, so I am very much obliged to you.' He pulls me up and takes my face in his hands and gives me a long, soft kiss on the forehead.

I feel as if I've been turned inside out and reborn.

I hear the door click open, and in the mirror see Spike, or is it Sam? Skip?? – staring open-mouthed.

Scorpio sees him too. 'Hi there,' he smiles. 'We're just enjoying some private time. I'll be leaving in a while.'

The guy opens and shuts his mouth a couple of times like a goldfish, then backs out and closes the door. 'Ooops,' laughs Scorpio, 'I don't know what he thought we were up to. I hope I haven't caused you to have a bad reputation. Don't worry about me though – I've already got one!'

We both shake with laughter as he hugs me against his chest.

'Oh man. I came here today thinking I'd be expected to ball that vicious old bag of bones. Instead I end up enjoying the company of a beautiful, natural, sweet woman. Thank you honey.'

He takes out his phone and punches in a number. 'Yay, bro, I'm ready to go. Yep. OK.'

'Oh, I forgot about your T-shirt. It's soaking. I'll have to find a bag to put it in.'

'Keep it, little lady. A souvenir of our time together, with my compliments. Do you realize I haven't even asked your name?'

'It's Alice,' I say.

'Alice. Alice. I'll remember you. You ever need anything, you just get in touch with me. Here's my direct number. Not many people have it.'

He pulls out a shiny white business card from his pocket with just an image of the Scorpio zodiac sign, and a phone number. On the back he writes: 'To my friend Alice, from your friend, Scorpio.' He adds a little squiggly kiss.

'Goodbye Alice,' he smiles. 'Thanks again.'

'Goodbye Scorpio.'

He pats my backside gently and walks out, closing the door behind him.

I stand in the tiny kitchen with my knees still shaking and my heart thumping faster than ever. If I wasn't clutching the dripping T-shirt against my belly, I'd think I was hallucinating. I lean against the wall for a few moments until my breathing returns to normal, then I call HR and say I don't feel well and have to go home.

Not wanting to risk passing the technical department in the basement in case I meet anybody, I switch on my full power and envision myself through the walls of the building, taking **Broomstick** back to my apartment. Being a witch has its benefits.

For an hour I lie on the bed with my eyes closed, reliving that unbelievable afternoon and wishing I could have recorded it to watch over and over again. If only people knew the real Scorpio. Behind his wild public persona, he's a kind, friendly guy. It was such a privilege to have him to myself for that brief time, and I will treasure the memory forever.

I stare at myself in the mirror to see if I look any

different. My face is still flushed with excitement and my dress and arms are still spotted with gore from Decima's nosebleed. Reluctantly I turn on the shower, and stand in the steam, rinsing away the smell of Scorpio's aftershave.

I hang his T-shirt on the curtain rail in my bedroom and will treasure it all my life.

4

Jealous guy

Sean

The studio looks like a murder scene. I grab Scorpio's silver jacket and race down the 18 flights of stairs, three at a time to catch up with him and Alice. I get to the production suite dripping in sweat. They're not there. Cory nods towards the kitchen at the end of the corridor. We all sit around waiting for them to appear.

The air fizzes with a strange tension. That's star quality for you, proof if ever it was needed that Scorpio's presence can be felt through walls. We all feel edgy about this guy. Nobody more than me. I planned on grabbing him right after the interview and dropping my new song onto him. Now the dongle feels like a weight in my pocket. I wrap my fingers around it one more time. This little sliver of metal could give me the break to the big time that I need. My song is good. It only needs to get to the right people, that's all it is.

The phone table in the center of the room is usually a mess. Covered with old scripts, running orders and half-empty coffee mugs but, weirdly, it's clear and polished. That'll be Alice, getting the place spick and span in case the special visitor comes our way, but how? How could she have known that he'd come down here?

The place feels darker than usual. Cory taps a foot over and over, Ramon flexes his arms, admiring his pecs; Josh chews slowly on some gum with his mouth tightly closed, a thoughtful, faraway look in his eyes.

I'm jittery. Now I'll have to approach Scorpio with my song when he appears. It won't feel so natural and everybody will see. I have his silver jacket over my arm. Shall I slip it into one of his pockets? But then I'd never know for sure if he got it.

The vibe is tense. It's not only Scorpio so nearby that's doing it. Decima is likely to appear at any moment. Fuming.

At last Cory says what we're all thinking.

'I was about to ask,' I say.

'A bit of blood on a T-shirt?' says Cory.

'What's taking them so long?' says Ramon.

'I'll have a look. I've got his jacket here.'

Josh says he'll switch on the security camera live feed if they take much longer.

Before going into the kitchen, I listen at the door.

Silence. A big radio silence, like they're not there.

I slowly pull the handle down. It clicks. I pause.

Nothing. I pull it right down and push the door open a crack.

I freeze, searching for something, *anything*, to say. I'll admit it, my eyes are glued to Alice. I see, no, *behold*, womanhood in all its perfection. I shut the door again fast, with a bang. I hope it's my mind playing tricks so I open it again. But no. There they are. Kissing.

Scorpio quickly finds his composure and gives me a triumphant smile. 'Hi there. I'll be leaving soon, when we've finished,' he says, cool as freaking ice.

I open my mouth to speak but no words come out. I nod, awkwardly, like I'm a ticket-inspector or something crazy like that, and reverse out of the door.

For half a minute I stand, taking it in, then after a few deep breaths I drop the jacket outside the door and race back to the edit suite.

The boys are watching them on the screen.

I can't cope with this a moment longer.

'I've got to stop this,' I say. Surprising myself. Where did that bravado come from? But, once outside the kitchen door, I can't bear it. I turn around, race up to Reception and collapse into one of the sofas opposite the desk. *What just happened there?* I take my time, breathe, breathe. I feel like a wronged lover and a wronged parent all at once. How dare he take advantage of that innocent girl. *Our* innocent girl.

The dongle burns a hole in my pocket. All it will take is a second, and it'll be in his hands, and then a few minutes of his time to play it to himself. And that'll be it. My fate will be sealed. But I can't think about that. I'm *boiling*.

Come on now Sean, concentrate. One quick moment and your song will be on its way.

I see the elevator wires moving. Scorpio is coming up from the basement.

I tense up and wrap my fingers hard around the dongle. Around my song. My future. But no, it goes straight past.

I wait nervously, watching the wires. At last, I see him through the glass. He looks serene, smug. This is it. I clear my throat, stand and, with a furtive glance across at the receptionist, I march up to Scorpio and grab him by his jacket collar.

'See here, man,' my face is as close to him now as Alice's was a moment ago. 'Leave that girl alone, OK?'

I give him an invisible but sharp punch in the gut.

He yelps like a puppy dog.

Before he can breathe in, I punch him again. Again. 'She's SPOKEN FOR,' *punch*

'OK?' *punch*

'She's MINE.' *punch*

Bang, bang, BANG in the gut. I swing him around by the shoulder and throw him out the door.

5

Tricky day at the office

Ramon

WOAH! Another day in paradise in the Tower of London. Or not! It isn't *the* Tower of London. It's called that because it belongs to a Brit, guy named Gauld. Never seen him personally. I'm just one of the guys working on the production of the TV show fronted by his daughter, Decima.

I wipe a trickle of condensation from the bus window as it bumps through town, bouncing on the potholes. This part of Hawk Bay City is a real dump if you ask me. Weeds coming up through the sidewalk, buildings boarded up, litter rolling down the streets. Why doesn't somebody do something about it? Why don't those people standing around doing nothing pick stuff up? Why don't they get the prisoners out to tidy the place up? It feels like nobody cares. There's no pride. When I get my break, the first thing I'm going to do is buy a decent place for my folks, somewhere neat and clean.

After a half-hour hot and uncomfortable ride I hop

off the bus and walk the last mile to my place, hitting the shower to wash away today.

They call me the gopher. I run errands and stuff like that, while I learn the technical side of things, but I always knew this job was more than that. It was made clear at the interview that I should stand ready and willing to service Decima on demand. It's written into my contract: 'The employee will provide any and all such services of whatsoever nature as may be required by the employer. Failure or refusal to do so shall lead to instant dismissal.'

No problem. I'm a red-blooded male, and Decima is a bitch, but she's an attractive one. Pleasing her is easy. I get more than enough sex to satisfy me and I don't go looking anywhere else.

This isn't my future. One day I'll be a megastar. See myself on the cover of Star Magazine: The 21st century James Dean! Had a few parts in a couple of Netflix series already. My agent, Maggie Chona, has been approached for me to do some 'adult' movies, but that could come back to bite me in future when I'm a big name, plus I'd be worried that my family would find out. My mom and dad would die if they knew what I do. We're a strong Christian family. Right back when I first told them I was going to be an actor, the first thing my mom said was, 'You're not going to let anybody see your naked butt. Ever.'

I don't want to brag, but I know I have the talent, and the looks – somewhere between Zayn Malik and Tom

Hardy, with my father's dark skin tone. Josh's pet name for me is Pretty Boy. Maggie is on it and gets me regular screen tests. She has total belief that I'll make it to the top, and says my strongest point is my versatility. I can play romantic and sexy, as well as vulnerable, or violent and brooding, and I'm pretty OK with comedy too. That gives me a load of opportunities. Stardom is waiting for me, I can almost touch it.

While I wait to be discovered, I need to eat and I need somewhere decent to live. I'm fastidious about personal hygiene. My friends will always let me flop, and I love them, but not enough to share their overflowing ashtrays or shower with their pubic hairs.

To rent a halfway decent pad around here costs big bucks, and that's the reason I'm here at The Tower, in a basement with three other guys, learning how stuff works when we're not obeying Decima's commands. It pays a whole lot better than flipping burgers, which is about the only other job available around here.

The other three guys are a good bunch; clean, because that's one of the requirements. Well groomed, good teeth, clear skin and 'well developed'. This job pays enough that I can afford to live in the style I like.

Josh is the director and special effects wizard. He's the oldest of us, laid back, patient, somebody you can talk to. I guess you could call him our father figure. If you were in trouble, he's the one who'd get you out of it.

Then there's Cory. I can't figure him out. For one

thing, he has this upper-class Brit accent, the kind you hear in old movies. Is that for real, or what? Sometimes I wonder whether there's another side to him. He's a – what's the word I'm looking for? – oh yeah, an enigma. A bit of a loner, always sloping off with his camera kit, or sitting in a quiet corner going 'OM'.

I dig his style though. His skinny frame carries all the black clothes well. He looks like a movie star and talks like an aristo. Decent guy.

The only one I hang out with sometimes outside of work is Sean. I go to church most Sundays, and it so happens Sean does too. We'll grab a beer together and watch a basketball game. We share our dreams and talk about when we both hit the big time, him with his music and me in the movies. We don't care that Cory and Josh laugh at our ambitions, because we know without any doubt that we are going to make it. One day they'll see how wrong they were.

Decima. She's a strange one. A gold-plated bitch with an insatiable appetite for sex. For my personal taste she's too skinny; I like a woman with curves, and with her money she could get that nose sorted out. Sometimes when I see her in profile I'm reminded of that bird with the huge beak – a toucan, I think it's called? And the teeth could use some whitening. Still, there is an animal quality about her that we males find a massive turn-on, so I'm more than happy being paid to 'provide service' to her whenever requested.

That is until Friday, when things turned pretty gross.

In mid-interview blood started running out of Decima's nose and dripping on her clothes. She choked on a glass of water and stumbled around, spraying bloody froth over the entire set, including her guest, Scorpio. I was hoping to have a word to see if he could give me some introductions into the movie industry.

Sean jumped into action, got Scorpio off set, and sent chubby little Alice, Decima's PA to clean him up in the kitchen.

Next thing we knew, Josh had switched the security camera onto the VT screen and we were watching Scorpio and Alice who seemed to be getting rather close. He tried to undress her but she played hard to get, so he backed off. To be honest I'd never taken much notice of her. She's a sweet kid, nice long golden hair and big blue eyes, but just not my type. But watching her now, for the first time I see there's more to her than I thought. Unlike Decima who is bold and full of herself and would have had Scorpio in her Passion Pit faster than you could blink, Alice is self-conscious and shy, yet she had the strength to reject Scorpio's advances. I was surprised. He's a very hot guy and no woman is immune to his charisma, but Alice stood up for herself.

All four of us were watching, but the VT had technical issues and kept flickering and blacking out, so we couldn't follow the scene all the time. Frustrating, but we had a pretty good idea of what must be going on.

When Decima arrived she was rigid with anger, and when she's shirty she's hot. She was also splattered with gore.

'Do your job,' she snapped.

The four of us did as we were told, because that's how we keep our jobs. I had to keep my eyes turned away from Decima to stop myself gagging, so I focused on watching what was happening in the kitchen. The screen was fuzzy for a while, and when it came back on Scorpio was kissing Alice, then handed her a piece of paper and walked out of the door, leaving her holding his dripping T-shirt. Then, get this: she vanished. Just like that. Poof! One moment she was there, the next she wasn't, she'd disappeared into thin air. Must have been a glitch on the security camera.

6

Into thin air!

Decima

I might have missed out on getting with Scorpio, *stolen* by my PA, but who needs a jumped-up singer when you got four guys who know exactly what you like? Each in his unique way?

Like I said, I've got these boys well-trained. I can't wait to get home. Home sweet home. My haven. My peace.

'Where've you bin?' demands Trevor as soon as I'm through the door.

'Where'd you think? But I'm home now aren't I?'

'Home at last!' Trevor shrieks.

'Cut it out.'

I'm pleased to see that Grant has laid the fire. All I have to do later is put a match to it. Running errands for me is beyond his job description, but he's curious about my little set-up here with my boys, and I make the most of his nosiness. I take Digby from my bag, give him a cuddle, peel off my clothes and hit the shower, locking the door against Trevor.

The warm, spicy smell of Estephe Gold fills the room. Our show sponsor is the deluxe make-up brand and I get an unlimited supply. Their cash pretty much runs the whole station but my show, with the celebrity guests, is the stand-out.

'Where are you?' Trevor calls from the other side of the door.

'Coming!' I pull on my robe, pad to the kitchen, pull a few snacks out and settle down at the counter on a barstool, followed by Trevor.

'Home at last,' he hops onto my finger and takes a sunflower seed from my hand.

'Yes, my boy. I'm here,' I purr and kiss his beak.

I pick up my phone but put it down again. I can't face it. Instead, I take Steffanie from where I left her last night next to the coffee machine and open the pages. I'm on Book Three of *Briarwood Witches*. It's so good. Have you read it? Maeve is such a badass.

I light the fire, grab some chocolate and zone out into dark magic and heartache. The Brit guy in this is so cool, nearly as cool as my Cory.

My phone plays a tune.

Trevor leaps into the air, squawks and starts flying around in circles. 'Get it. Get it. It's for YOU. Get it. Get it.'

My heart sinks. I expected this, but sometimes it's better you don't know what you don't know, if you know what I mean. I might as well get it over with.

'Hi darling,' he says.

'Daad,' I return the fake fondness.

What's this smarmy attitude about?

I stand at full height. 'All right, before you start…'

'Chaos. *Chaos*, Decima. I've never seen such a mess of an interview. Do I get an explanation? Why didn't you call me?'

'I was busy.' I hit the speaker button and dig into the fire with a poker.

'I bet you were,' he sniggers.

I pout, blow Trevor a silent kiss and roll my eyes.

I wait for the explosion. The last thing I expected from him today was a laugh. A cheap joke, but all the same, almost friendly. I don't trust it and wait for him to erupt.

But, instead, there's a long pause.

'Are you not pleased to hear from Daddy?'

Oh this is so tedious. I really can't be bothered to go through the motions with him.

'What do you want?' I hold the glowing poker up to the light.

'Now now.'

'What is it?'

'The ratings are going nuts, Decima.'

'At my expense.'

'Never mind your expense. If it pulls in the pounds for me, it's making you more famous by the day, and you know it.'

'Dollars, Dad. Dollars,' I say slowly. 'Where are you anyway?'

'Not sure. ORNELLA – Ornella, where are we?'

I hear my sister muttering in the background, my poor big sister. Permanently locked to his side. Who'd be a pet daughter? What an escape I had there.

'You're nowhere near Lorelei Thornheart's ratings yet.'

I don't reply. He loves to bring her up at any opportunity. When I'm starting to feel really settled, too. I'm doing a great job of faking it. I hate it when he does this. I have power too. I'm a strong, powerful queen bitch and the last thing I need right now is to be reminded that he's the one with the power. Pulling the strings from somewhere. Wherever he is.

'So, where are you right now?' I repeat.

I don't really care where he is. I don't think he cares either. As long as he's in his plane he's happy. If I ever do want to know what's going on, I simply get Ornella to feed me the intel via the pilot. There's no such thing as a trustworthy private jet pilot. They are the biggest gossips with a network that stretches, literally, across the world. Each has his intel price. If only more billionaires running dodgy deals knew that they'd be safer slumming it in First Class. I'd never tell Dad that. Why should I? What's he done for me other than adopt me, steal my inheritance and then screw up my life?

Maybe he's simply flying around in circles above us here on the East Coast, with Ornella trotting backwards and forwards providing for his every whim.

He's not interested in women. Or men come to that. I know looks can be deceptive, but not here. The only things to bubble his piggy pink skin up with the sweats are the dollar deal and his blessed private jet. Making money, in other words. And looking like he's making money. Preferably by crapping on somebody from on high. Literally. It's not a pleasant thought. Now I can imagine him sprawled in his calf leather suede seat that matches his vomit-colored corduroy suit, stomach straining his shirt buttons. The worst thing is, he thinks it's a cool look. Like the Aviator sunglasses and crocodile square-toe shoes when all it screams is oily operator, keep your distance.

I'm ready to put the phone down, but then I hear the name Alice Archer in the mix and my ears prick up. He wants my help. What kind of help?

7

'Let's find you some gauntlets'

Alice

Last night I slept surprisingly well after all the excitement, and today I'm going to visit my parents. The sink is piled with dirty dishes. I flick a *Clean* spell so they can wash themselves. Why waste time and energy when you don't have to!

Mother will have stacks of food for me to bring back. She always does so I travel conventionally, using public transport and carrying a large backpack.

There's a bus stop right outside the front door of my apartment building, but as the bus will either be very late or not arrive at all I stroll along to the railway station. The subway would be quicker but no! You won't catch me down there, locked in a metal tube and not knowing how long the oxygen will last.

The train is only eight minutes late and not overcrowded considering it's a weekend. I find a seat opposite a boy plugged into his phone, jerking his head to some kind of metallic noise leaking out of the ear buds.

He puts his feet up on the seat beside me. I catch his attention, smile at him, point at the boots and raise my eyebrows in the hope he will take the hint. As he chooses to ignore me and stare out of the window, I summon the **Tickle** spell, which creates a persistent irritating itch to the sole of his left foot, and for good measure I drain his phone's battery.

I amuse myself watching him trying in vain to scratch his foot without removing his Doc Martens, and then search without success for his charger. That's when I plug my phone into my own power pack. He leans forward and taps my knee and signals to ask if he can borrow my charger, but I point to my ear buds to indicate I can't hear him. I spend the rest of the journey studiously watching the passing countryside. I'm a nice person, I really am, but certain things like bad manners bring out the mischief in me. At times like that being a witch can be useful.

When the train pulls into the station, I let him find his charger where he had frantically searched several times, in the pocket of his baggy jeans. His face is a picture of puzzlement. I catch his eye and wink.

Smiling to myself, I walk the two miles to my parents' isolated house, kicking up the crispy fallen leaves and breathing the cold sharp air. I love this place, the wildness and peace of the terrain compared to my life in the city.

I could of course have **Broomsticked** from the station, but it's a delicious fall day and I enjoy the rare luxury of time to myself. My work diary for next week looks hellish. Decima has already been bombarding me with emails and WhatsApps, despite company policy that employees are not to be contacted over the weekends, but then Decima is a law unto herself. It's her time of the month, when her infinite venom really hits the fan and spews effluent at warp speed 8. I'm not going to let that prospect spoil the next 48 hours. I'm looking forward to a good lunch and spending quality time with my parents.

I arrive at exactly 10.45, which is the time we have mid-morning coffee and fresh bakes at the weekend. Clambering over the travel crates and sacks of wood shavings in the hall, I find my mother, who is also a witch and prefers me to call her Astrid, in the kitchen pouring coffee and arranging cinnamon buns on a tin plate. I squeeze my rump onto a pine chair already accommodating a ragged cushion and a heap of gardening magazines, and help myself to a handful of buns. The aroma of coffee mixes with the smell of a sickly sweet air freshener that does not entirely mask a distant whiff of something sour.

'You know those plug-in smelly things are bad for you, don't you? Full of chemicals. Why don't you make something yourself?'

'You're quite right. I should. I will. One day.'

Astrid places a mug in front of me and perches on the table. Her plump arms are covered in lacerations and spots of dried blood.

'A new litter?' I ask.

She nods. 'Yes. Penelope's first. Eighteen in all. Large for a first time. Most of them are sold already. Drink up and we'll go and have a look.'

My father, Patrick, puts his head round the door. His hands and clothes are splattered with paint.

'Ah, Alice,' he says.

'Hi Dad. How are you?'

'Fine, thank you.'

Astrid kisses him on the cheek, hands him his mug of coffee, and brushes his mop of hair off his face.

'How's the painting going?' she asks.

'Fine,' he replies, turning and closing the door behind him.

'Come on,' says Astrid, sliding off the table. 'Let's find you some gauntlets.'

8

Screechers

Alice

My mother pushes aside the heavy kitchen table and pulls up the trap door leading to the cellar. I follow her down the metal steps and along a dark corridor until we reach a reinforced steel door. She dials a number into an electronic keypad and the door swings into a glacial cavern. From behind a further steel door comes the sound of growling, snarling and something sharp scraping on metal.

'Bless them, they're hungry,' says Astrid. As short and rotund as she is, my mother is immensely strong. She hauls a sack of pork chops out of a cooler and heaves it over her shoulder.

'Open the lock, Alice,' she says.

I wind the wheel on the door until it grinds open and we are met with a cloud of frozen air and a cacophony of blood-curdling noises.

Astrid turns and smiles proudly. 'Listen to that! And they're only six days old.' She tosses the meat through a raised hatch behind a network of iron bars, and the creatures pounce upon it, clawing at each other.

I have never shared her enthusiasm for the Mottled Screechers she's been breeding for the last 20 years. I grew up hearing the shrieks and yowls of her breeding stock and watching her treating her scratched arms with the special oil she makes. Once she was careless and didn't notice me toddling behind her. I was almost snatched through the bars by a tom. And don't get me started on the stench.

Astrid has three passions: my father, her garden and these creatures. She loves me, but I'm not a *passion*. Her Mottled Screechers are in demand worldwide by *autre monde* aficionados of Screechfights. She can't breed them fast enough. Watching her training them I'd been sickened by all the blood and gaping wounds, but as soon as she bathes them in the healing solution they are instantly repaired. I still think it's barbaric.

It isn't the sale of the Screechers where she makes the real big money – it's the *Salvheal* she's developed over the years. Originally she'd tested it on herself and once or twice on me when I'd fallen and scraped a knee or entangled myself in the brambles. It is literally magic, regenerating lost ichor and torn skin in a few seconds. Oh how big pharma would like to get their hands on it.

Four minutes after she pushed the meat through the door, the only sound is a loud synchronized purring.

'Come with me,' she says. 'I want to show you

something.' She fiddles with the keypads again and opens a door to one side, stepping into a warmer room.

'I'm not touching them,' I say when she hands me the gauntlets.

'Shh,' she says. 'I need your help.'

In the corner of the room on a leather pad lies a tangle of fragile bones and wrinkled skin. It could be a frog, or something a dog has sicked up.

She picks it up and places it in my hands before I can snatch them away.

'It was the last one born. Penelope rejected it and the others attacked it. I've healed the poor thing as best as I can, but it's very, very frail. I haven't the time for it, so I thought you could see if you can help it. I'd hate to lose one.'

I stare at the ugly little creature, hairless, eyes closed, ears drooping, drool leaking from its mouth. It's small enough to fit in an egg cup.

'No,' I say, 'I really can't look after it. There's a no-pets at work rule, and in my apartment.'

But Astrid is already pressing the keypad so the door is sliding closed. I briefly consider tossing the lump back onto the cushion but my soft side gets the better of me, and I fold it gently in the gauntlets and follow my mother back to the kitchen. I wrap the Screecher in a soft flannel and tuck it into my cleavage.

I inherited my curvy shape from Astrid and my height from Patrick. It's probably my permanent unquenchable appetite and weakness for Parmesan cheese and Baileys that gives me a certain amount of padding around my middle and thighs.

Lunch is the best meal I've had all week. At work I'm too busy to eat, and once I get home I'm too tired to cook, so I mostly eat junk and chunks of Parmesan. Whatever else Astrid lacks in household management and maternal skill, she makes up for in the kitchen.

My father joins us at the table.

'So Alice, how are you?'

'Great, thanks, Dad. How are you?'

'Fine' he says.

Which for my Dad is quite a conversation. He turns his attention to his plate and eats methodically, chewing each mouthful rhythmically before swallowing. He's an engineer, and does everything with precision. Somehow Patrick and I have never managed to develop the deep father/daughter bond you see in films and TV dramas. My father is kind to me in a slightly vague way, and I've always felt he tries to love me but something holds him back. I love him anyway.

I remember when I was ten, asking my mother 'Why doesn't my dad love me?'

'Of course he loves you,' she said, 'he loves you very much.'

'Then why doesn't he talk to me, or hug me like other dads do with their kids?'

'That's because he's English. They're different to us.

Englishmen are reserved; they don't show their emotions, but believe me, your dad does love you. You have to accept that he doesn't know how to show it.'

And so I do. But sometimes I wish he was more demonstrative.

He reminds me of Cory, who's English too and I can never tell what he's thinking. He always has that same expression on his face, as if his mind is somewhere far away.

Maybe it's also because I've inherited Astrid's magical powers. The fact that Astrid is a witch and breeds unearthly creatures in the basement is my father's dark secret. I think he'd hoped I'd be born 'mundane'. He's always been worried that I'll do something wild to draw attention to the family, although I've never done anything at all spectacular, just little mischievous things that nobody would really notice. I did once change the salt for sugar, so he ended up with rather sweet spaghetti. I watched the puzzlement on his face and had to stop myself from giggling. Astrid flashed me an amused look and raised her eyebrows. I would never do anything to hurt anybody.

'Enough with all this witchery stuff,' he'd said. 'We're not living in the 17th century. If we were, you and your mother would both be hanged. Study hard. You can have a decent job, a secure future, a normal life.'

I did try. I tried design, I tried engineering and I tried IT. The harder I tried, the more I realized a good job and a normal life didn't appeal to me. I couldn't adapt to the routine and the discipline of studying. I was suffocating until I noticed a small ad pinned to the notice board in the college hallway.

It didn't say much: 'OPEN-MINDED AND ADAPTABLE PERSON TO WORK IN UNUSUAL ENVIRONMENT. Call 0776522'

I called. Two months later I was working for Lorelei Thornheart, the witch who was Decima's predecessor. My father thought that was his worst nightmare, but it was nothing compared to what was to come. Now his daughter is working for a notorious, self-proclaimed exhibitionist nymphomaniac.

I scrape out the remains of the mushroom pie and creamed potatoes, and help myself to two slices of cheesecake.

From the depths of my cleavage a small movement reminds me that I am hosting a life. I peer down into the darkness where the Screecher is feebly waving its miniature clawed hands.

'What does this thing eat?' I ask.

My mother produces a plastic pot of black paste from the fridge. 'Give it a pinhead sized blob on your finger every two hours. Careful it doesn't bite.'

I cautiously poke my finger down at the small ugly face as it licks the stuff slowly, then emits a pungent fart.

'Do you think it will survive?'

'Unlikely, but you never know. It's worth a try.'

Yes, I think rather sourly. As long as it's not you trying. But to be fair she is always busy with the breeding and exporting programmes and the time-consuming process of *Salvheal* manufacture, as well as tending her beloved garden and keeping my father well fed. She gives a little secret smile when she hears him say that he married her for her cooking. If he only knew the truth! A pinch of her own *Nyum* powder makes any dish irresistible. 'I'll do my best', I promise.

I have no idea how I'm going to raise a Mottled Screecher, nor what to do with it while I'm at work. Nor do I plan on feeding it every two hours, and in the unlikely event that it even survives, what will I do with it when it starts to develop its naturally horrible habits?

On the other hand, what else do I have to pass the time after work? My social life is virtually non-existent, and I'm getting increasingly bored with *The History and Future of Haiku* which was a recommended read in the culture column of *The Hawk Bay City Herald*. I'm trying, but to be honest I don't really understand any of it. I'm halfway through and thinking that life is too short to read something you don't enjoy, but on the other hand it seems lazy to give up. Nurturing a weird creature will give me a good excuse to put it aside. And anyway, I must admit I *am* lazy.

'You should name it,' my mother says. 'Positive energy to help it in its fight for life.'

'I'll call it Zylch.' Because it probably has zilch

chances of surviving, I think.

I leave after tea, full of apricot tarts and Victoria sandwich with raspberry jam, as well as one of my mother's 'tonic teas' which she feels I will need over the coming days.

I mention the difficulties I'm having with Decima at work, so she takes a small bottle from the pantry and tucks it into my bulging backpack.

'Keep this handy. It will calm her down. Be careful not to give her more than a single drop at a time, though. It's extremely potent,' she says with a little wink. I check the label: *Dorm*

I hug her goodbye at the gate, then she turns and walks back into the house without looking around, closing the door behind her.

9

Brief encounter

Alice

With the weight of food in the backpack, and the awkwardness of carrying the creature between my breasts, I decide to take the quick way home. As much as I try to stay mundane, there are times when a little magic helps. I click the **Broomstick** App on my phone and select 'Medium' speed because sometimes I get giddy if I travel too fast. I'm home in a few seconds.

By the way, you're possibly wondering about the **Broomstick** phone App, so I'll explain.

Broomstick itself is a powerful travel spell, but it has a serious flaw. You can't control the speed it takes you, and this has resulted in nasty accidents in the past. Witches shooting over the edge of cliffs, into trees, or into crowds of people, knocking them down like skittles and involving the police. It also has a tendency to break down, leaving you stranded.

A group of witches and wizards came up with the idea of using modern technology to make it into a phone

App, enabling improvements like speed control and secure arrival.

The older generation won't use it. They are firmly against the introduction of technology into witchcraft, regarding it as a dangerous step, and fearing that it will 'get into the wrong hands' – meaning muggles, as they've famously been coined by Ms Rowling, people without magical powers. By the way, please don't take 'muggle' as an insult. It's only a word to distinguish between people with magic powers, and those without. Can you think of a better word?

Actually there's no danger of that happening, thanks to the clever App designers, because the App has two modes. Muggle mode users can make virtual visits anywhere they choose around the world to enjoy the sights and sounds. Only witches and wizards can toggle the App into magical mode to use for convenience and accuracy to travel wherever they want to go. It's quite expensive, but I was lucky to get a free copy as I tested the Beta version.

As I walk up the stairs to my apartment, I pass somebody coming down. I press myself against the wall to leave them room, but they turn and go back up, saying 'Please, after you'.

The voice makes the hair on my arms stand on end. I look up into a face so beautiful it takes my breath away. Large soft brown eyes fringed with long black lashes; a narrow, straight nose, pink lips curved in a gentle smile, a cleft chin and shiny black hair lying in a cowlick on his forehead.

He stands aside at the top of the stairs waiting. For a few seconds I am paralyzed, staring up at him, and then I edge past, conscious of the bulk of the backpack and the odor of Screecher poo coming from my T-shirt.

When I turn to thank him, he's gone, leaving me engulfed by a feeling of overwhelming loss. My nostrils catch a faintly exotic scent that I can't identify.

After I've unlocked my door and dumped the backpack I find a small Tupperware container, line it with kitchen paper and carefully extract Zylch from his nest. He makes a feeble and unsuccessful attempt to bite me as I feed him the black gloop, then I lay him in the bowl and cover him with one of my old fluffy socks. Leaving him snarling gently and scraping his teeth with his claws, I start to unpack the backpack and load the freezer. I put the small bottle of *Dorm* in the bathroom cabinet, and then spend the rest of the day arranging my furniture the way I like. When Rory was here he was always moving everything a fraction of an inch this way or that, and wiping away imaginary dust.

The memory of that fleeting encounter on the stairway kicks in and I open the door onto the hallway. That intoxicating perfume is still drifting faintly in the air. Coconut and spice.

10

Confused

Cory

I get home from the studio, head for the fridge and grab a beer. I neck it in one, open another and slam it down on the table.

My mind is a mess. And I don't do mess. Keeping cool and calm is my thing. Envy has got me again. The one evil I thought I'd banished from my life for good has come sneaking in the back door. First Scorpio, then Sean. Double envy. Imagining what our Sean and Alice might be doing was worse than having to see her kissing Scorpio so enthusiastically.

The longer Sean was gone, the more I imagined. What were they up to? OK so Sean wasn't with her. But I know he wanted to be. Now I've got a fight on my hands. Ramon and Josh weren't thinking any different to me either, and Sean is ahead of us all. Come to think of it, Josh may be as crazy about her as the rest of us but he's not going to go there at least. At his age coping with Decima must be enough, and he has kids Alice's age. He's all set here with Decima, they seem to have a strong link of convenience going on.

My eyes settle on the back yard. The winds have knocked over the palm pot again. Damn. I check my FitBit. I have an hour or so before the sun goes down. Still as Lake Placid out there. I finish my beer, slip into my old crocs and go out the back.

'Now Mr Palm, behave, OK?' I squat down, grab hold of the pot handles and heave. I'm careful, I don't want to put my back out again. That affects everything. If I can't service her properly, Decima gets ratty with me and I get even more furious with myself.

What am I doing in this life here?

Maybe I should simply go back to England and fight for what's rightfully mine? An image of my brother comes to mind and I curse him. Then myself. All the mindfulness and meditation in the world isn't going to take the problem away. Live in the moment, Cory. Back to the moment, boy. That's all you can do. For now anyway.

The pot finally yields and when I've shoved it back into position, I scrape up the earth that's fallen on the fake lawn. I take my time, letting the sandy grains sift through my fingers. My mind turns to the acres of rolling green hills and valleys, dotted with forests, surrounding my rightful home. I love the feel of the earth in my hands. Earth is real wherever you are. Earth is honest. And what am I? Neither of those things. I'm no better than this nasty fake grass. I need a way out of this crazy life that's so cushy and easy on the one hand, and so evil and wrong on the other.

Why didn't I get to Alice before Sean? I return to the kitchen, fill a watering can and take a slow turn around my yard.

I try to concentrate on the moment, but it's hopeless. I'm tempted to reveal all. But now I've walked away and left karma to do its thing, what would it be worth?

Oh, by the way, Alice, I was never a butler. I've escaped the English aristocracy. How come? My twin brother grabbed our inheritance all for himself. That's what three minutes can do for you. Three minutes older is all he needed to lord it over me. Have you ever wondered where that expression comes from? It could have been invented for me. He didn't need the full three minutes. One minute. One second would have done it. But, you know what? My karma, and my pride, is intact. What's a castle, a title and a private income worth if you have to live with your own actions? Who needs all of that?

To attract the girls, you idiot! No, no, no, to attract the one that you love. That's what! But no. Not Alice. I should be ashamed to even be thinking of such crass posturing. I hate myself today.

My phone buzzes. Blast. Decima's still fired up and is summoning me. She's insatiable. But, actually, I'm up for it. What else would I be doing tonight except mooching around fretting? Trying, and failing, to meditate it all away.

On the drive over to Decima's, I double down on my gut feelings. It wouldn't work anyway. Alice is far too pure to be impressed by titles and possessions. She'd think I was crazy anyway. That all the drugs of my past had got to me. I must keep my secret, from Decima especially. If she knew the truth I'd never hear the end of it. It's bad enough having to hear her brag about 'her' English butler on the crew. I must win Alice's heart the right way, the honorable, honest way. But how?

11

Zylch

Alice

Tonight Shelley has a date, so I'm babysitting for her. We met at college and immediately bonded. Being dyslexic, she was struggling, and so was I, being 'different' from the other students. She's my only close friend. She married young and had two kids before she was twenty. He left her soon after the second one was born. She's devoted to her little girls. Her life revolves around them and seeing her with them makes me feel good. She's a natural mother and I'm fascinated watching her care for her little ones. My mother never had much time for reading stories and teaching me to bake, so it's a novel experience for me.

I'd really love to be a mother like Shelley. But first I'd need a husband, and I'm 25 with no boyfriend.

If only Shelley could find Mr Right and settle down with somebody who'd make her a good husband and be a father for the girls. She's pretty and funny, and I know there will be someone out there for her if she can find them.

She lives on the other side of town. It's not the nicest area. There are a lot of homeless people there, living in tents and makeshift shelters. I can't imagine what it's like not to have a place to live, being out on the streets through the bad weather.

When I travel through town I like taking public transport, and especially the bus. You get to see what's going on, and sometimes you can listen in to people's conversations, which can be interesting. The subway is quicker, but as I said earlier, you won't catch me down there.

Zylch didn't want his food this afternoon. I'm a little concerned. I've wrapped him up to keep him as warm as possible and put him in my bedroom where it's quiet. I'll only be gone for 4 hours. I thought it would be better for him to stay there, rather than taking him with me to Shelley's. I've never taken any interest in the Screechers so I really don't know anything about how to look after them, but this tiny creature has tugged at my heart. It's so ugly, yet so needy.

I've had a great time with the kids. Now they are tucked up in bed, I've grabbed a chunk of Parmesan and poured a glass of Baileys, and sat down to watch a Scorpio film, the one where he teaches a blind woman to dance. Oh my goodness, he is so beautiful, and has such a kind face. No wonder women of all ages adore him. I still wonder if I imagined what happened down there in the kitchen.

I munch my way through the cheese while I'm watching the film, and end up with tears streaming down my face and crumbs of cheese down my cleavage.

After I leave Shelley's I'm walking back to the bus stop when I hear some shouting and see a couple of feral youths kicking one of the homeless people who is curled up on a sheet of cardboard.

I summon my power and cast the *Ouch* spell. The homeless person becomes a concrete block that smashes into the toes of the kids' trainers. They yelp in pain and hobble away as fast as they can. I smile to myself. The concrete block becomes once again a homeless person sleeping as peacefully as it's possible to sleep on a sheet of cardboard.

When I arrive back at my apartment I check on Zylch. There is no movement from the naked, wrinkled body. I lift it out of the absorbent cotton and it lies cold and stiff in my hand. I've let Zylch die. Tears spring out of my eyes, roll down my cheeks and drip off my chin onto the little creature. I hold it against my heart and sob and sob until I have no more tears left, then I fold it back into the absorbent cotton.

I find a velvet-lined box that had held a bracelet and lay Zylch gently down in it. Seeing his tiny body lying there makes me cry all over again, and my tears splash down onto him. I wipe my eyes and close the lid of the box. Tomorrow I will bury him. I scrape out the jar of black paste and rinse it down the sink.

I'm too upset to eat anything, so I crawl into bed and drift into sleep.

I'm woken by a strange sound coming from somewhere in the apartment, a rhythmic scratching noise. At first I think it is the branch of a tree tapping at the window, and then I remember there aren't any trees outside the window. Maybe it's a bird on the sill looking for food. I ignore it for a while but when it doesn't stop, I climb out of bed and follow the noise to the living room. I switch on the light and look around for the source of the noise. On the side table the small box is rocking back and forwards, and the noise is coming from there.

Trembling, I lift the lid and see Zylch, reaching up to me with two tiny hands. I scoop him up tenderly and hold him to my cheek, feeling a flutter of heartbeat. He's alive.

I sit with him in my hands, watching his limbs squirm and his eyes beginning to open. It's the first time I've really looked closely and I see a pointed upturned snout, small round eyes, drooping Spaniel ears. He is making gentle murmurs and opening his mouth. I begin crying again, tears of happiness, and as they splash onto his body his naked skin begins to develop a pink tinge. It seems less wrinkled, smoother, healthier.

I remember I flushed away his food and he must be desperately hungry. Surely there must be something else he can eat until I can collect more food from Astrid? Perhaps yogurt? Carrying him in the palm of my hand I go to the kitchen.

I'm not the tidiest person and the fridge is a bit of a mess. To reach the yogurt I have to take out the orange juice and leftover risotto from the night before last, and a packet of mushrooms, a jar of peanut butter and a piece of Parmesan I brought home from Shelley's.

Zylch twitches in my hand and rolls onto his stomach. Clinging to my finger he pulls himself upright, murmuring excitedly. I place him on the table and he crawls towards the food and tries to climb up the peanut butter jar. He wriggles around it scratching at the glass with his little claws.

I open the jar and dip my finger in and hold it out to him. He grabs my finger with surprising strength and laps greedily. He feeds hungrily for a couple of minutes, then after giving a discreet burp and fart, purrs contentedly and rolls himself up in my hand with his tail wrapped around his head like a harvest mouse.

My heart swells. When I wake at first light of morning, he's curled up next to my pillow, and Scorpio's T-shirt is hanging from the towel rail.

12

She's the one

Sean

I'm not an aggressive guy. Truly I'm not. But I'm a jealous guy. I'll own that. I grab my electric skateboard from the front desk. The security guard looks at me with vacant eyes and a slight smile as he hands it over.

With a quick nod of thanks for the blind eye to my violent outburst, I get out of there. Ah well. It's nothing he hasn't seen before.

I feel sick. The useless dongle is a weight in my pocket.

I plug my earbuds in and look up at the sky. It's a clearer blue than it has any right to be on a day like this. I drop my board down with a loud clatter and jump on. I'm sad all right about the lost opportunity to get my song out there. I'm fuming. I should have punched him harder.

And lower down.

I glide along the gently sloping hill towards the bridge and head for downtown. I'm so tensed up. Each judder of the skateboard rattles every bone in my body. I want to cry. I feel so sick I throw up into my mouth. I swallow it back down again before I even think about spitting it out. Me? A cool muso like Scorpio? A guy that gets the girl? Who am I kidding?

At the bridge, a warm breeze picks up from the river and blows through my hair. A flock of gulls rise up from the tarmac, shrieking angrily as I pass. Ha, that's more like it. The distraction clears my mind. I'm cool again and I know exactly where I'm heading.

There's only one place to go when I'm feeling like this. My heart lifted, I turn up the sound and roll on down to Main Street.

I take a left at Martha's Candy Store and cruise towards Jerry's Bar at the west edge of town. Regina Styles sings her high 8 octaves sweetly in my ears.

I speed through every stop-light, my eyes narrowed, avoiding direct eye contact with the alchies and no-hopers hanging outside the stores.

Liquor stores are everywhere in this town, only outnumbered by Cliff Gauld's Candy Stores, and we all know what kind of under the counter sweetie trade is going on there.

At least those liquor stores are doing what they say they're doing.

I don't complain. How can I when I owe Gauld, the owner of all of those bow windows and doors that ring that fancy tinkle when you open them, my job. My life?

And Alice. My woman! Not mine yet by a long

thread, but she will be. Soon. These deep feelings don't spring out of nowhere without a reason to be there. And where I'm going now will speed that along a little. I'm going to need all the help I can get moving into a relationship with Alice because there's competition.

I need to be first out the traps because I'm *not* sharing her with the boys. Oh no.

Decima, yes. Alice, no. Alice is the *one*.

That's where it all comes from isn't it! All this romantic malarky about being The One. Who'd ever have thought it. It's the honest truth of it! *You're the One* I hum to myself. I click Regina off and hum. *Oh You're the one, My one and only one, You're the one…* Where did *that* riff come from? It's good! I sing it over and over to myself so that I don't forget it.

I saw the way Josh, Cory and Ramon were all melting for her too. How could we all be so *dumb*? Servicing that bone-faced crow all this time. What's a long pair of legs compared to real beauty. Inner beauty? Soft beauty that's been staring us in the face but hidden from us all this time. Decima isn't going to like it, but I can't care about that now. *Oh you're the one, my one and only one, you're the one.*

The terrain gets more tricky for electric skateboards the more west I get. I have to work to keep my balance as I swerve the holes and tufts of grass growing out of the cracks. There isn't another workout like it and I love it.

La, la laaaa… de wah wah wah. The song for Alice is forming all on its own, it's coming down from the sky and

I'm in heaven. This is way better than the song in my pocket. Poetic justice? The luck of the Irish? I can feel the wheels beneath my feet, rumbling over the concrete is keeping me grounded, but man, I'm spaced. Simply thinking about her. The name. Alice. Alice. Alice. It's so beautiful. What a *name*. What a day! What a song!

What a day, the day I fell in love with you, what a day…. When all my dreams came true…

On impulse, I take the dongle out of my pocket and throw it into the gutter. That was the wrong song. And that was the right move.

I feel euphoric.

I take a left by the empty lot at the pike, glide past the row of derelict brownstones. The tarmac has crumbled to dirt. I'm juddering along now, every bone in me rattling away. I jump off by Jerry's Bar, and sing the melody into a voicenote before it's gone.

Jerry's looks shut. Jerry's always looks shut. There's boards nailed across the windows with graffiti and old peeling posters all over. I take a left down the side alley… now I can hear voices, laughter, the chink of glasses coming from inside. Jerry's has always been the best speakeasy in town. I'm tempted to go in for a quick one, but I wouldn't be proud of myself if I did, for it wouldn't be the one glass would it? I'd still be there at 10.00 tonight, and besides, I'm on a mission.

Behind Jerry's there are two flags, the Stars and Stripes and a Jolly Roger, criss crossed together and flapping in the breeze above a narrow door. I can hear grunge music playing. Not my thing, but still. I hop up the steps to the door, black and peeling, that's seen better days. It's on the latch. I find myself in a familiar hot, dark space that smells of solvent and that smoke you get after you've lit a match. I barely catch my breath when, out of the shadows, Tom appears.

'Hey, man. Long time no see!'

TomaHawk, the coolest dude in Hawk Bay City if ink is your thing. Now Tom is a sight to be seen, even in this light. It's easier to say what parts of him are not inked, designed and got fancy piercings through than what are. If the honest truth be told, that's nothing more than his eyeballs, I swear. And he's probably googling ways to do that every time his wife gives him any time to himself.

'OK Tom, I'm here for something special. Real special now.'

He blinks, beams widely and follows my eyes down.

I nod. 'You know what I'm meaning, Tom?'

'The forty-nine pincer?'

I nod.

'Man.' He laughs and slaps my back. There's never nobody more happy than a serious tat man hooking up with another serious tat man.

I follow him out back, grinning like a kid at the circus.

'Prick or balls?'

'Prick. With letters runnin' up the side… A name.'

Tom raises his eyebrows, setting off a chain reaction

of piercings moving about his face.

'Top side or under?' he says.

'Under what? Oh I get you, man.' I blush, which doesn't do nothing to hide my ignorance. I think for a minute. I can't go too crazy. I need some discretion here to keep my main job servicing Decima. For a while. Until my music takes off.

'It'd better be underneath, Tom, my man. Just the five letters…

'Shout them out, man?'

A.L.I.C.E..'

13

Tension

Ramon

Oh dear, poor Sean. He's got it bad, bad, bad in a big way. He's fallen hard for Alice. Seriously fallen for her, I mean, not messing around. He never takes his eyes off her and follows her like a lost puppy. I saw him watching Cory chatting to her. He was clenching and unclenching his fists and had a face like thunder.

She is such a sweet kid and I reckon if she was more self-confident and less timid she could be a real looker, with those big blue eyes and blonde hair. She's great at her job, but she needs to lift her chin and put her shoulders back.

Decima gives her a hard time, but she shakes it off, so she must be tougher than she looks.

This morning I walked up quietly behind her and put my arms around her waist, shouting 'Boo'. She screamed and turned around and couldn't stop laughing.

Then Sean appeared and snapped at me to get back to work. Uh oh!

14

Escape into nature

Cory

I'm leaving the production suite for a shoot when Alice appears out of nowhere. She *keeps* doing that!

How?

I lift my camera-bag above my head as we squeeze past each other in the narrow corridor, pausing in unison for a split second as our paths cross. That's when she peers up and throws me the sweetest, kindest look you've ever seen. A bolt of electricity shoots up my spine. The glint in her eyes is ambiguous and electric. Like, *she knows* it's us. It was always meant to be us. We simply haven't acted on it yet. I stay standing right there like a stupid statue and watch her sail away from me towards the kitchen. I close my jaw, lower my bag sheepishly and swap glances with Josh, who saw it all through the open door of the production suite. He's got a WTF expression all over his face. I lick my finger and draw a 1 in the air.

One up for me, I grin.

He doesn't smile back but turns to his work. I am not

smiling inside either. Who am I deceiving, if not myself? This whole Alice thing is driving me insane.

The four of us have supposedly come to terms with it. There is some sort of unspoken agreement about how things are now. We all feel the same and we know it. Since spying on her with that cocky singer, we've all fallen under some kind of spell. She seems unaware of it, which only makes her all the more desirable. Is it *because* she's so innocent that we've all been pulled in with such force? Because of our… unusual life with Decima, maybe? Is it nature calling us back to what should be the truth in any adult relationship? Which one of us will win the race? We take it out on Decima, who's getting more enthusiastic treatment than ever, and she hasn't a clue why. Which does make me smile. These thoughts preoccupy me all the way to the car. I'm still enjoying the afterburn of that hypnotic, split-second moment in the corridor. A glow. A warm, heart-lifting, glow. Did I imagine it? No. Josh saw it too. Am I the favored one? I throw my camera gear rather heavily into the trunk.

Stop these foolish thoughts! I stand for a while watching the elevator sliding smoothly up and down the western side of the Tower. The clouds are so low today that they're reflected in the glass, turning it opaque and sinister against the mist. I move to close the trunk, but instead grab my gear for a few shots.

I send the drone camera up into the air. I swear it's got a mind of its own, this tower. Perched out here on this fog-laced promontory like some kind of slick Manhattan sea-monster that's lost its way. It's an odd thing for a recluse like Cliff Gauld to build. Such a statement. Or maybe that's the point. He needs to get his rocks off somehow I imagine. Nobody's been in his life, as far as anybody knows, since his wife died soon after they'd adopted Decima and her sister. If he had found a new wife, the National Enquirer would have told us. It must be tough for Decima and I feel for her.

I shiver. With loneliness, the cold or both? What the heck, I fold the car roof down all the same. I need clarity. Driving around the city looking for visuals always cheers me. I love my camera. I love the opportunity Gauld has given me here. Whenever anything is troubling me, any time, day or night, out I go, looking for shots.

I drive over New Bridge, as it's known. Built by Gauld as one of his fake good deeds for the city. The old bridge used to lead to the community center. A refuge for this city's many, many drug addicts. As soon as New Bridge was up, he blackmailed the federal council key players and dynamited the center to build the Tower. He's that kind of guy. I've never met Gauld, thank goodness. Everything goes through Josh.

I always hold my breath until I'm safely over the other side of the bridge. Rumor has it that it's full of dynamite. If the Tower of London is ever threatened, Security can press a button and the whole thing will explode.

The guilt never leaves me. Why do I work for a monster? I defy you to look the other way when you see a Facebook job ad scrolling by one day, when you're on your uppers in a foreign country, with a headline that says *FREE SPIRIT WANTED.*

Creative trainee cameraman. Top pay. No qualifications needed beyond an open mind.

That caught my attention. I came to the US to become a basketball pro. But injury put paid to that. I was getting plenty of work, hamming up my upper-class British accent, butlering at fancy dinner parties whilst I thought about what to do with the rest of my life. Going downhill rapidly seemed to be the best option for me in this city of unemployment and drugs. I was saved in time by rehab at a meditation center. I got so into it, I was even considering the priesthood…and then… well, this… One of those universe things that's surely meant to be.

In many ways being a part of this team is my ideal job. The boss is never around. Always a bonus. He leaves us to get on with it. As long as Decima is regularly serviced and the show keeps its ratings, it all runs smoothly enough.

I truly believe that nobody owns anybody or anything. They only think they do. So the weird request that came with the CGO TV crew job couldn't have been more up my particular Acacia Avenue. I thought it was a prank at first. And then I met the guys. They're a great bunch. We're all live and let live free souls, helping each other out. Sharing one, non-possessive, woman. Our physical needs are well-met and we all get on with our lives. But now this whole possessiveness vibe is creeping in. Despite all the work on myself, it seems I'm as grabbing and selfish as the next guy.

I turn left over the bridge and head towards the fancy gated communities on the shoreline out towards the Interstate.

I have grown to love this strange, lawless city. There's a special kind of desolate beauty to it, especially out here on the windswept fringes. The bleak, vast horizons and enormous skies are like something out of a film. An old road movie, maybe, or a Western. You could simply drive on forever. I'm grateful that I have found a place to belong. I feel more American than English these days, enjoying the kudos my Englishness brings here. And yes, I suppose I do play on it. The butler thing. Who doesn't love a butler after all? Insisting on Yorkshire tea rather than coffee (I get the tea bags shipped) is all a bit of an act. Well, it fits the job. I am still 'in service' to Decima. To give is to receive. It's that simple really. And I'm getting to go out and film scenery, GVs as they're called in the trade, General Views, for the show. It's creative and I love it. Truly this is the perfect job for me.

I speed up and keep my eyes straight ahead as I pass Eagle's Nest gated community, Decima territory. There'll be enough of her later. I'm soon speeding along the A4 Interstate South with the wind in my hair.

Thirty minutes down the road I'm parking in my preferred spot by the beach. Away across on the distant horizon the sun is struggling to get through the sea mist but it doesn't stand a chance.

After taking a few shots, I place my camera gear safely up the beach, strip down and run to the shore. I lie down on my back with my head facing the waves, stare up at the sky, and let the waves wash over me.

Breathe. In for two, hold for four, out for six. Relax. Whoa. The water's so cold! Nearly killed me a couple of times, I have to confess, but that's a part of it. After the troubles that my birth brought, being reborn is important to me. I never know what's coming next. As with anything in life and, believe me, there's nothing better than drowning to clear away troubled thoughts.

The worry about the next wave coming takes over from everything else. Usually. But today that's not what's on my mind. Alice. Yes. But what concerns me the most is the way we're all bickering with each other now. Without actually fighting, like, it's under the radar. Like that odd look from Josh. That stupid, cocky sign I gave him. Why did I do that? I *hate* possessiveness. In myself most of all.

I give myself a reality check. Whatever my feelings, I'll always be in her friend zone. I may be many things, but I'm not stupid. How could I ever end up with her when Ramon and Sean are fighting openly to get her attention. Even Josh, at his age, is less of an outside contender than me. Don't ask me why. I know it. I let them get on with it. But then again… that smile, that look. I don't, do I? They do say that hard to get is the biggest aphrodisiac of them all. *Do* I stand a chance?

You see.

That's what I mean!

She's driving me crazy.

The harmony between us boys is under serious threat. That's the truth of it. It's all innuendo, those glances, those wink winks here and there. The only time we're as one is, ironically, when we're with Decima. We know exactly what we're doing there. Like a well-oiled four-part harmony machine. For a while, we forget about our silent battles for Alice's attention. And, yes, for all that I say, I'm still a contender not out. It's bringing out the old sportsman in me.

Decima's enjoying our change of gear at least. She's about the only one I reckon.

WHOA! That's insane! As if it heard my thoughts, a big wave just washed over me right down to my thighs. I leap to my feet, choking, spitting out seawater and laughing hysterically. I shake myself down like an old dog, hike up the beach to my gear and get to work. Soaked, satisfied, reborn and ready to go.

The drone gets a fantastic wide shot from here right back to the Tower, swirling in its own mist, with the city beyond in sharp focus. I take a few more shots with the still camera on zoom before setting off again. It feels like my luck is in, good shots usually come in clusters so I keep my eyes peeled for the next one. When I reach the main city limits I pull over and dig my laptop out of my bag. I need to get these beauties over to Josh to edit into tomorrow's graphics. Stings, they're called. You see them at the beginning of every news show and before every ad break.

Josh is always ready to go the extra mile to get the best sequences. He works his magic with my images, twisting them into spirals of graphics and words, then Sean adds his sounds. We're the best. We're winning every award going. Things aren't so bad! The sessions with Decima aren't unpleasant I have to say. It's part of the job. What I was hired for.

15

Coup de foudre

Alice

Decima has been more spiteful than ever recently. All day, every day, she's sniped and criticized everything I do. The latest thing is about my hair.

'Do you really think it's appropriate, Alice, to have your hair dangling everywhere while you're working? I'd rather you tied it back – we don't want stray hairs getting everywhere.'

I've been wearing it loose since that day two weeks ago when Scorpio came to the studio. I like the way it feels. Cory overheard Decima, and he whispered to me: 'You keep it like that, Alice.' And that's what I'm going to do, whether Decima likes it or not.

I've tried to concentrate on my job, but my nerves are pretty jangled.

When I went to work for Lorelei, my life changed. Although by then she had become a mega-star, she was a kind and gentle person, who took me under her wise wing. Being shy by nature, at first I was over-awed and timid and didn't think I could handle the job. I was used to spending most of my time alone, studying, then I suddenly found myself in a hectic environment, trying to understand technical issues and dealing with celebrities who could sometimes be very difficult and often reduced me to tears. Lorelei was always calm; she praised me and encouraged me, and comforted me when I screwed up.

She was almost like a mother to me. My father was furious. He thought she was going to encourage me to develop my magic, and that I'd be throwing spells all over the place and drawing attention to the family. Even though that never happened, he was always hoping I'd find a different job.

I don't know if Lorelei knew about my powers. It was something we never discussed. I didn't mention it, and if she felt it she never said anything.

Over the three years I was her PA my confidence grew. I learned how a TV studio works, and how to manage people. I loved my job and was gutted when Lorelei left so suddenly.

She was cool with it, though, because she went off to LA and became an even bigger star. We keep in touch. She still sends me a gift on my birthday, and at Christmas, and has invited me to visit her any time. I miss her.

Working for Decima can be grim.

I know what you're thinking. Why would I work for somebody so horrible?

I did think of quitting when Gauld fired most of the

old crew and replaced them with guys more to Decima's taste, if you get my meaning.

As it's turned out Decima's 'stallions', as I call them, are all really decent guys and I get on well with them. We have a lot of laughs. I love the buzz of the studio and the people I get to meet. Even though I had to take a pay cut I still earn more than I could anywhere else in town. No other job would give me the same pleasure and satisfaction.

It was touch and go whether I kept my job. After Decima had interviewed me, I overheard her saying to Gauld: 'She doesn't seem too bright, but we might as well keep her for now. She could be useful. I'll have to move her down to the basement though. Couldn't have her scuttling around me all the time.'

Gauld agreed I was too useful to lose. He'd dropped Decima into a role she knew nothing about, and he'd fired all Lorelei's technical staff except for Josh. I was the only person who knew how to bring everything together for the programme.

I called Lorelei and asked her advice. Should I stay?

She told me to go for it, but to make certain to have a watertight contract because, she said, they'd keep me as long as they needed to and then kick me out.

Lorelei put me in contact with a lawyer. 'He's a slithering snake,' she said, 'but trust him. He'll look after you.'

She was right. The only way I can be fired from here

is with a bullet. Gauld read carefully through the contract when I put it in front of him, then signed it as if it was of no interest and pushed it back at me. He underestimated me. If he'd known I'm a witch, he'd have been more careful and if he ever read through it again, he'd be surprised to see what he'd agreed to.

My guess is that Decima is not a happy person. She may have the glitzy lifestyle and the fame, but nobody who's happy would be so mean. Being forced by Gauld to take the job must have been hard on her. It was bad enough that she had no experience of working in a studio or presenting a programme, but she also has to pretend and make viewers believe she's a witch. That's a heavy load. Before that she was an aspiring actress who was going nowhere, and her 'job' had been testing sex toys.

If only she were nicer to me, I could help her so much.

Weighing up the pros and cons, she's the only bad part of my job. All the rest is great.

How long is she going to be able to make people believe she really is a witch? Once they know the truth, she'll be finished. So will my job, I guess. It's funny, she has no idea I know she isn't a witch, and she has no idea I really am a witch. How freaked would she be if she knew!

My father was cross when he learned I was going to stay on after Lorelei left. He had hoped I had 'got all that silly stuff out of my system' and would go back to college.

He and my mother are horrified and ashamed that I'm now working for a self-confessed sex addict. I know my folk want the best for me, but their idea of what is best for me is not the same as mine. Even with Decima's nastiness, I still love my job for the most part and I want to hang on to it for as long as I can.

This Saturday morning the weather's mild and sunny, so I decide to wander down to the harbor. I shared my breakfast with Zylch – peanut butter and jelly on toast. He's strong enough this morning to hold crumbs in his paws and he's visibly growing. He doesn't stink as badly as he did, which is a blessing, as I've tucked him down my cleavage so I can take him with me.

Much as I love this town, it has to be said that the crime rate is pretty high. There's a big problem with muggings by addicts wanting a fix, and you need to keep your wits about you all the time. I never carry anything that could attract attention, and I don't wear expensive jewelry because I don't actually have any.

I sit on the harborside with a coffee. There's always something to watch, it's relaxing, lively and busy with the chatter of the crowds. The air smells of the sea, diesel from the motor boats and mixed aromas from the food stalls.

I feel Zylch's body pulsing against mine and close my eyes, enjoying the sun on my face and the memory of Scorpio. Something to one day tell my grandchildren if I ever marry. I'm so chilled I'm almost asleep when I hear a scream.

Opening my eyes, I see a skinny man attacking an elderly woman and trying to snatch her purse and shopping. She's fallen to the ground and is clinging with all her strength to her shopping bags. I leap up and run towards her, at the same time hurling **Affliction,** which causes the attacker the painful stomach cramps that herald an attack of diarrhea. He grabs his belly and frantically runs towards the bushes.

(**Affliction** is a spell I find particularly useful, as it's adaptive. I don't need to choose a specific action, it does that for me, afflicting the person according to what it feels is the most efficient way to stop their behavior quickly. You may remember that it caused Decima's nosebleed when she was preparing to humiliate Scorpio during their interview.)

The woman lies on the ground moaning. I squat down next to her and see she has scraped her elbows. As she struggles to sit up a pair of golden-brown hands reach out and help her to her feet.

I gather her scattered shopping and stand up, aware of the sweet scent of coconut and cumin.

He's there, the man I passed on the stairs. Looking into his face, I'm hit by a *coup de foudre* – lightning strike.

He brushes down the woman's jacket. She thanks us both and goes to collect her bags. I touch her raw elbows lightly with a healing spell and the skin is instantly repaired. The man frowns slightly and looks at me.

'Have we met before?' he asks.

My throat is dry, and I croak, 'We passed on the stairs at my apartment a couple of weeks ago.'

The woman thanks us again and continues on her way.

'Ah yes. I thought I recognised your face.' He smiles. 'Fancy meeting again like this. So you live at Bentley House apartments? One of my colleagues lives there. I think you were coming up when I was on my way out.'

'That's right,' I reply.

'Well, have a nice day,' he says, looking at me for a few seconds before walking away, then turning back and raising a hand.

I feel empty, drained, shaken. I want to run after him. I want him to hold me in his arms. I tell myself I'm being ridiculous. You can't feel like that about somebody you've only just met. Can you?

To make myself feel better, I buy a giant bag of French fries and a pot of mayo and sit on a bench watching the boats moving around in the harbor. Zylch stirs from the depths of my cleavage, so I break off a morsel of potato and push it down there. I feel a movement as he reaches for it, and see a woman sitting opposite me giving me a strange look. I smile to myself, imagining her telling her friends 'And she was poking bits of potato inside her clothing'.

By late afternoon a cool breeze wakes up and wraps itself around my bare arms, so I stroll back to my apartment. I notice a figure standing beside the entrance. I mentioned before that there's a lot of crime around the area, so I'm on my guard and ready for trouble.

As I reach the entrance the figure turns towards me with a smile.

'Hi again. I hope you don't mind, but I was wondering if I could take you for a coffee? I'm Jai.' There's that intriguing scent of coconut and cumin.

16

Unwelcome news

Decima

My phone is on loudspeaker, leaving me both hands to crash and bang pans about the kitchen.

Dad is freaking out about some new kid TV reporter on our rival station TWC.

I yawn, listen and wait. Trevor comes and sits on my head.

'Don't you dare poop, Trevor.'

'What was that?' he shrieks.

'Nothing, Dad.'

He's fuming. If there's a button you don't want to press with Dad, it's publicity. Nothing odd there with his way of doing business. Apparently this young journo has done some special about the scrappy piece of land on the edge of town called Brent Flats that Dad has got his hands on.

'So, how *did* you "acquire" this land?' I ask in all innocence.

'Shut right up and listen. This is serious.'

Backhanders and bribes. Nothing new then. I put my

phone down on the counter and let him rant.

'Come and sort it out!' I bluff, calling to my phone from a safe distance, as if he could suddenly whoosh through the screen and appear before me like an evil Genie.

I can't help smiling at the explosion of expletives that come back to me. Hiding from everything, he barks down instructions from his ivory tower, literally, in the skies most of the time. Flying around so much that nobody can pin him down. On anything.

'If you're that worried, sell it on. What do you want that piece of wasteland for anyhow? We've got enough car parks full of weeds in town.'

'Golf.'

'*What?*'

'My golf club.'

'But nobody plays golf around these parts.'

'I do. Or, I will do.'

I'm speechless.

'Hello? Hello? What are you doing there?'

'Cooking.'

'You don't cook.'

'I'm learning.'

'Take me off speaker right now.'

'Only following in your footsteps, Dad.' But I do as he says. I don't want him to spontaneously combust in mid-air after all. Not yet anyhow. I let him ramble on.

'So put out some of your good news do-gooding PR.'

That's his usual way. Paste over the latest dodgy deal with 'good works' for the community. He's almost as secretive about 'his' charities as he is about the intricate web of money laundering connections that keeps it all churning over. There's usually some ulterior motive behind the 'it's all for charity' line anyhow. Such is the way of business deals the world over.

'This journo is an ambitious little creep, he's going after me big time.'

'So, take it to the next stage, bring on the threats.'

'It's not working,' he says in a freaky, squeaky kind of strained whisper.

'And what am I supposed to do about it?'

'He's going for the jugular…'

'Stop the project then!' I yell.

'Then he's won, you idiot.'

I'm losing the will to live here. 'OK, carry on then. Carry on flattening houses and replacing them with holes filled with sand to build some mad golf fantasy that nobody round here wants.'

'*I* want it, Decima.'

There. He's said it again. Could he be retiring? Moving here? I feel sick. That would mean Ornella too. I can live with not being the favored one, but not if my sister is in my face with her pretty, pretty frocky, sad pouts and cheesy blonde curls. Supposing, then, one of the boys took a fancy to her? I can imagine Josh, the dirty, adorable old goat that he is… But no, it's not going to happen.

'I need some local intel on this flashy journo Rex Tillman, he's got to be muted.'

'So, tell me first, what has she got to do with this?'

'Who?'

'My PA!'

'What are you on about?'

'You know, Alice Archer, the one I inherited. The one I *didn't choose*. You mentioned her when we last spoke.' There's a pause.

I wait. I'm dead curious.

'Her family have the last house over at the Flats.

'Ahh OK.'

The country club site.'

'Oh it's a *Country* Club now?' I laugh. 'It's not a country club, Dad. It's a piece of wasteland.'

'Country *and* Golf Club. You ever heard of landscaping? It won't be anything unless we can get them out.'

'What do you expect me to do about it?'

'Find out why they're digging their heels in. They've been offered decent money to leave. They're being difficult, that's all. And get me the lowdown on Rex Tillman.'

'But you know all there is to know.'

'Street gossip. I need to keep squeaky clean legal on this final eviction now. Find out where he got his tip-offs.'

'It could be any one of those city officials because they're all lying thieving crooks, Dad. Just like you.'

He snarls out a string of expletives and the line goes dead.

I'm disgusted with myself. At the end of the day, I'm no different to Ornella, am I. A puppet adopted daughter, jumping to his command. But at least I have my perks. I go to click my phone off but change my mind. Sean. Sean has his ear to the ground when it comes to the media bars of this city.

I hit Sean's number.

'Sean. Sean, *Sean*, pick up.' I feel the power returning to my voice.

I switch to repeat call. He still doesn't pick up. I change tack and start purring into his Voicemail

'Sean, honey, I need you, now. I need phone sex. NOW.'

17

The wrong woman

Sean

Oh no, Decima. Not now, woman.

I look down there and all I'm thinking is it'll never rise again. Sore doesn't begin to describe it.

In one way, though, I guess I'm ready for Decima at a distance, walking around my apartment naked as the day I was born. Can't have anything near my privates, nothing touching. The thought of boxer shorts gives me the shivers, let alone them tight revealing things Cory wears.

'To be sure, I will so!' I say in my exaggerated Irish accent that turns her on so much, grimacing to the wall. 'Give me five! I'll be getting my toys out to get *real hot* for you, Decima.'

I hang up.

Now what? I don't know how I'm ever going to have sex again when I'm healed, heck, with *anyone*. But that's alright, I'll be waiting until Alice is good and ready.

I have to catch my breath as a warm, glow flits up from my heart at the mere thought of her. I can tell you, Cupid's real! As real as day! Who'd ever have thought it?

I close my eyes and imagine our first time. I think of Alice's tender smile, her delighted surprise when, as we're about to make love for the first time, she discovers her name spelled out on my tenderest spot. But no, it's not that is it? I shake my head at my own stupidity.

This is IT.

I'm surprising myself here, but there it is, I don't want to sleep with Alice, do I. Well, that too, but more than anything else in the whole world, I want to kiss her.

Kiss those soft, dewy lips and look into those blue, blue eyes and have that trusting soul connect with mine and know that our warm bodies will be as one, together, always. Loving. Caring. Living as one unified soul. All the marriage bunkum you hear folk talk about is suddenly ringing true, loud and clear.

I gaze into the air with a faraway smile. This is it. That madness all the books and films go on about. That thing that turns once lonely souls into loved-up bores.

I'm in love. I got it full and bad and I haven't even got a photo of her on my phone yet.

I open my eyes and look down at the new ring on the tip of my privates, glinting in the sunlight pouring through the window as if it's winking directly at me. I'm telling you, once you let him in, Cupid's every place you look, firing them arrows off.

'What about when Alice discovers YOU for the first time?' I ask my flaccid, sore little man.

'This is yours,' I'll tell her. 'For you. And you alone.'

Maybe that's the wrong way round. Maybe I should present her with a ring. The engagement ring, before she sees this one. Maybe, maybe we should wait until we're married before we go there? That's what I was brought up to believe. Father Jonathan would be proud alright. We could fly back to St Aidan's in Kilkenny. That's the romantic way of doing it isn't it. The right way round. I mean, we needn't wait long. It can be a quick engagement. We'll be ready… Or maybe we'll be wed here and then have the blessing in Ireland later, when we can afford the trip?

I gently lift my little man up, imagining her face when she sees her name. This ink hurts but, believe me, it's good hurt. Knowing her name is tucked safely away there brings me out dizzy, to be honest.

Oh no. Here we go. Like a Pavlovian dog, I give in to my phone's beeping.

'Sean!' Decima's shriek jolts me back to the here and now. I get straight down to work.

'Getting meself all right and ready for you my darlin…'

'U huh?' she whimpers.

'U huh, too right I am.' I pick up my jeans from the bed and make some noises with the belt and buckle. 'I'm oita my jeans, oh, darlin, if you could only see me now. I'm uh uh so ready for you. Are you ready for me, honey?

Silence.

'To be sure, I think you've gone all shy on me

Decima. Is that so now?'

That's what she does on the phone. It's a funny thing so it is. She goes all coy and little girlie. This isn't the Decima anybody but me knows about.

After a few minutes' dirty talk, I hear her panting down the line. Then she says it.

'Oh oh oh. I love you Sean.'

Says it every time. She doesn't mean it. Only ever says it on our phone sessions when she's in this weird little girl mode. She's not capable of loving, that one. Cupid's given her a wide berth.

'Now you don't go telling anyone about us, you hear, Decima. This is our secret.'

'Yesss. Seanie. Our secret love. I love you so.'

To be fair, secrets *are* sexy and usually do it for me. Not this time. I listen to her making all sorts of noises. It won't be long now.

At least it's always all one sided. She doesn't ever even try to give anything back. She'll shut her line down any second now.

Except she doesn't. She stays on.

'Sean?' she purrs.

'Hmmm,' I say brightly. What's this about now?

'You drink with that journo Rex Tillman who leaked the problems about Dad's land deal, don't you?'

'U huh,' I say noncommittally. 'I see him around the place. When he worked at the Tower we'd have a bevvy or two together. His sister would join us sometimes. But not any more.'

'You're friends with his sister?'

'Not at all. I think she did fancy her chances with me, but, well why would I be interested in her when I've got you? I haven't seen her in years.' And that's the truth.

'What's her name?'

'Jan, works as a hairdresser at the Store.'

I don't know what's coming out of Decima's mouth next and I'm on full alert here. A part of all the acting I have to do to keep my job sweet. I should be a member of the Oscar Academy Union.

'How do you think he got the info?'

'Why are you asking me?'

I change the phone to my other hand and start pacing. What's this about?

Tillman was another of us trapped in her father's snare. Keeping the news interesting and promoting the boss's business at the same time was an impossible situation. I always felt sorry for him.

'He did a good job when he was with us. It could be revenge for the way he was treated when he was fired.'

'But *how*? How did he get the information about the golf course? Nobody knew that, Sean.'

'Clearing them slummy houses? It's a joke isn't it. Some vanity project. Some official it would have to be? That district attorney would be heading for a big bonus there, I'm guessing, if he could clear the one house left standing.'

I keep the talking going. Not telling her about the rumors going round Jerry's Bar that Gauld's going to send the heavies in anyhow, on the quiet. They'll show no empathy for that family, whoever they are. I'd hate to be in their shoes right now. They don't know what's going to hit them.

18

First date

Alice

Jai asks if I have a favorite place. I've never been invited out before. Rory didn't believe in spending money unnecessarily and I wouldn't venture out on my own, so I say I'll leave it to him to choose somewhere. I expect him to head for one of the busy, noisy places on Main Street, but he turns off there to the eastern part of the town center. It's the better part of town, cleaner and more prosperous. Where the professionals live.

We walk side by side. He's relaxed and chatty, I'm wound up like a spring inside, but doing my best to appear cool, as if being out with a devastatingly handsome man is something I've been doing all my life, and not for the very first time. I catch passing glimpses in the shop windows; an elegant, bronze-skinned man, and a tall curvy girl with long blonde hair, wearing a baggy tracksuit. We do not look like a well-matched pair.

You smell Mumtaz before you reach the carved turquoise doors with the name picked out in gold lettering. The fragrance of coffee and spices floats down the street, drawing you towards it. Jai opens the door and lightly touches my back as he guides me in, sending an electric shock up my spine.

There's a warm, mysterious ambience, incense floating on the air, low, haunting music playing. It is so different from the modern, glass-fronted places we passed on Main Street. The lighting is low, peeping through carved arches on the turquoise walls. The seats are deep and richly upholstered in vivid blues and ruby reds, inviting you to sink into them, to feel at home, to stay as long as you like. It feels like walking into a jewel box or a prince's palace. I'm looking for the right word. Exotic, that's it. Like a distant, foreign country.

Jai hands me the menu. I don't know much about coffee. It all tastes the same to me. We have machines at the Tower, I drink what comes out of them. Astrid brews fresh for my father; it somehow never tastes as good as it smells. Decima only drinks Black Ivory, which she says is made from coffee beans pooped out by elephants. I don't believe that; who would drink something that comes out of an animal's backside? She says it costs more than I pay in a month for the rent of my apartment.

'Can I have whatever you're having?' I ask.

'Sure,' he smiles. 'But I don't drink coffee myself. I'm a tea drinker.'

'Uh, I've never had tea, but I'll try. You choose for me, please.'

He signals to a waiter and murmurs a few words. The

waiter returns a few minutes later and places a tall glass cup in a fancy silver holder in front of each of us. I raise it to my mouth and take a sip. It's hot, sweet, mildly spicy and creamy. A taste sensation.

'Wow,' I say. 'That is so good! What kind of tea is that?'

'Where I come from it's known as cha, or chai. Black tea, mixed with spices, sugar and milk. It's a big part of our culture.'

'Where is that?'

'In the north of India, in the Punjab. It's where my family lives, where I was raised. Our family business is textile production.' He smiles wistfully.

As soon as he mentions his family, I feel a pang of sadness. If his family lives there it is where he'll surely be returning.

I've gulped my drink down greedily, and Jai glances at the waiter and passes a silent message that results in another glass of chai arriving for me.

Zylch wriggles about deep down in my cleavage, and I pretend to scratch my belly in an attempt to settle him down.

'You must miss home,' I force myself to say.

He nods slowly. 'In many ways I do. We are a big family, and we're very close. The Punjab is beautiful, wide-open spaces, and a nice climate. Not generally such hot weather as other parts of India. Never as cold as it is here,' he laughs.

'Why would you want to come here then?'

'Because,' he starts, 'I felt the need to know more about the rest of the world and find my place in it. Life in my community can be restrictive. My family are very religious Sikhs, and as much as I love them and my country, I'm not ready yet to be tied down. My interest is environmental sciences. I'm working with a local organization researching ways to protect the remaining unspoilt marshland here. Our world is changing and we need to learn how to change with it, but we also must protect it. That's my aim.' He shrugs.

'But please forgive me. I haven't even asked your name. Tell me about yourself.'

'There's nothing to tell really. I was born near here. My parents live out on the Brent Flats. My father is an engineer and my mother is a...'

What do I say about my mother? That she has magical powers and breeds unearthly, vicious fighting creatures and exports them all over the underworld? He'll think I'm crazy.

I continue. 'My mother is a sorceress and breeds Mottled Screechers, a kind of cross between feral cats and dragons, bred to fight.'

'Go on,' he says, smiling.

'I work as a PA to Decima Gauld, the TV presenter, in that hideous glass monolith down by the harbor. And my name is Alice.'

Jai tilts his head slightly and says: 'Pretty name. I like

it.'

An hour goes so fast and he signals for the bill.

'I'll walk you home,' he says. 'And thank you for keeping me company today.'

We are strolling back to my apartment when the oddest thing happens. We're on Main Street, when the floor manager from the station comes towards us, the cheerful guy with red hair, always whistling. His name escapes me. Steve? Stu? Sam? Buck? Spike, that's it. He's just dropped his skateboard onto the sidewalk when he looks up and sees me. His face breaks into a huge smile.

'Alice! How great to see you! What are you doing downtown?'

I'm mildly surprised by his enthusiasm. We hardly know each other apart from sharing a few smiles at work.

'Oh hi,' I say. 'How are you Spike?'

'It's Sean,' he grins, taking a couple of steps towards me, then he notices Jai by my side.

'This is Jai,' I say.

Jai holds out his hand politely, and Spike stares at him for a moment, then says: 'What the hell!' His pale face flushes bright red.

He glares at us both and scoots away.

'Is that a friend of yours?' asks Jai.

'He works at the station,' I say. 'I don't really know him. Embarrassing, because I can never remember his name!'

Jai shakes his head with a small smile. 'Yes, it

happens. He seemed to know you though.'

I'm planning a way to invite him up to my apartment without sounding desperate, but when we reach the entrance he holds out his hand and says 'Thank you again, Alice. You've been lovely company. I've enjoyed this afternoon.'

And before I can open my mouth, he's turned and walked away, leaving me gaping like a goldfish running out of water.

I watch until he turns the corner.

19

Alice on my mind

Josh

Well darn! What's with Alice? Since the Scorpio episode she's been positively radiant. There's a glow of happiness around her, a new confidence in the way she moves. I'm having erotic dreams where she's the star of the show.

But poor kid, I hope she doesn't think she meant anything to Scorpio. Still, it's great to see her looking so happy. She's certainly got the attention of all of us now. The mousy PA has become a testosterone magnet, she doesn't know it yet, that's all.

I put those thoughts out of my head. I couldn't take advantage of a naive kid like her. What she needs is protecting. I'll take her under my wing, and make sure no harm comes to her. I've seen the others licking their lips, and I'm not going to let them hurt her.

20

Confusion

Alice

From being the reluctant caregiver to Zylch, I've become the doting surrogate mother. Each day he grows in size and beauty. He's as big as my hand now and covered with a silvery fluff. His snout is longer, and he's a demon at sniffing out food, as I discovered when I went down to the store and left him in the kitchen. He found the Parmesan and gnawed his way into it until his tummy was full, then he fell asleep on his back with his legs in the air. His paws have become more like human hands, with neat, rounded nails instead of claws and his little tail curls upwards over his back. He really is the cutest creature, nothing like Mother's vicious fighting monsters. She'll be surprised when I take him to visit next weekend.

It's been a bit weird at work. Decima's boys have suddenly all become really friendly and supportive. I haven't any idea why, but from being the almost-invisible woman, I'm apparently flavor of the month. I find flowers on my desk, boxes of chocolate and sweet little notes. Why this sudden interest in me? Sometimes they flirt a bit, which I admit I do enjoy, but it's only a bit of fun. When I close my eyes it's Jai's beautiful face that I see – his long-lashed sincere eyes, glossy black hair and those lips that I so badly want to kiss me.

On the other hand, Decima seems to become more vicious every day.

The Floor Manager with the red hair – the one I bumped into on my first 'date' with Jai – has asked me out a couple of times. It's quite funny – he was gulping and flushing bright red. He looked so crestfallen when I politely refused. He seems very lonely. Maybe if he asks me again, I'll have a coffee with him to cheer him up.

Jai has invited me out again – twice. There was an exhibition of neolithic paintings at the Art Museum. To be honest it isn't something I'd choose to visit. Although my father is something of an artist – he paints and sculpts – I'm a philistine when it comes to art appreciation, but I'd go anywhere to be with Jai. Literally anywhere.

Once we got there, I actually found it interesting. Some of the paintings are really quite beautiful. We spent nearly three hours and had a coffee afterwards. A couple of weeks later he was waiting outside the apartment building when I came home from work. He asked me if I'd like to go out on Saturday. I said I'd love to go to Mumtaz again and drink chai. It's a small place and we have to sit close together.

I'm confused. We get on so well. He's interesting and he's interested in me. We laugh a lot. I want to reach out and take hold of his hand. Well, actually I want to throw myself into his arms. But something warns me off. He has never touched me, never held my hand when we walk together, never says he'll see me again. He thanks me for my company. I don't know how it works. Should I make the first move? That doesn't feel right. Maybe it would scare him off. I think it has to come from him. If I see him again, I'll invite him up to the apartment and see what happens. I think about him all the time. Literally all the time. When I see him my heart lurches.

Now that Zylch is bigger and able to feed himself, I can leave him in the apartment while I'm at work, although he seems to be going through a clingy stage. Once or twice I've come home and found the place trashed – the curtains and sofa chewed and the contents of the kitchen cupboard spilled all over the floor. I tried an experiment last week – transforming him into a pot plant and keeping him on my desk, but people began looking at me very strangely when I took it home every night, and then Cory came in while I was talking to it. My latest idea is turning him into a scrunchie and using him to tie my hair back. It's worked but by the end of the day he gets restless so it's better to leave him at home.

The Floor Manager – his name is Sean, not Spike, as he's reminded me a few times – has been walking in a strange way the last few days. A bit bandy-legged. I asked if he'd hurt himself, and he went very red in the face and said he thought he'd trapped a nerve in his lower back.

The other guys smirked, so I imagine it's something to do with his visits up to Decima's office. I know exactly why they go there and that's cool. Not my business. Live and let live.

21

Viral spiral

Decima

I look at the name on my screen in disbelief. Ornella? What does she want?

'Yes?'

'I'm so so sowy Decima.'

'Don't you start.'

'But it's, it's simply so tewwibly AWful for you, Decima.'

'What do you care?'

'If you put it like that, Deccy, not tewwibly tewwibly, to be perfectly honest, we've been virtual stwangers all these years haven't we, but Daddy's, well, to put it mildly, he's blown a fuse, more like a gasket actually.'

What's a gasket? 'Ah so he's put you up to this. What's it about?'

'You have to fix it, he says. We're being made a laughing stock, Deccy.'

'OK right, tell him I'll ask Twitter to kindly shut down for a few weeks. There's nothing to be done, Ornella. You have to let Twitter storms die down on their own, like real storms, until they're forgotten.'

It all started with a Tweet.

A few lines of words scrolling past a few hundred eyes.

If that witch @CovenStar229 up in Toronto hadn't shared it to her 135K followers, it would have been forgotten by now.

But no. The clip of my nosebleed went viral. Then it became a Gif and Scorpio started using it for his own ends, sharing it to his 14 million followers. Hoping to get traction for his feeble new song. Then every coven of bitch witches across the State hopped on. If I was a real witch, that would never have happened is what they're saying. What's this bitch doing screwing her guests and bringing the good name of witches down? Not like Lorelei Thornheart, there's no real ghosts on THESE shows. Lorelei's the #realdealwitch #notthisbitch.

So the news is out. I'm not a real witch. Then it got worse. They discovered that I'm the owner's daughter and the vitriol went off the scale. The owner's daughter… nepo baby writ large.

The latest in the viral spiral comes from the International Union of Witches' Rights. I'm taking the job that a real witch could and should have. So they're challenging me to prove that I'm a witch. #proveitbitch is the hashtag. I'm keeping quiet. That's what you do with Twitter, you let it eat you up, chew up your insides, take away what sanity you have and if you're not dead by the end of it you pretend it never happened and carry on.

I think back to that morning. The way Scorpio was distracted, Alice coming closer and closer. It's not @CovenStar229 though, is it, who started this? It's that little madame in the basement.

Now this. My scraggy sister. All fake empathy and frills.

'I gotta go.'

'No – wait. There's something I wanted to share with you, Decima. There's a weason poor Daddy's so worked up. The thing is… OK I'll simply say it, you know Pilot Towin?'

'No,' I say to wind her up.

'Daddy's pilot.'

'Never met him.'

'You know OF him surely…' she gives a fluttery laugh.

'What's your point? You found true love outside daddies and teddies?' That's a bit of a low blow, even for me, considering my own Digby Bear is my precious fur baby.

'We have become close, yes. But that's not it. The thing is… well Daddy's in tewwible twouble, everything could come cwashing down at any moment. And this whole Twitter thing could be the last stwaw, the thing that bweaks us all. Towin's a bit of a double agent, a spy, like James Boond, you know…'

'Bond,' I sigh.

'You see. He knows 100% Wex Tillman has got talks

with a pwoduction company for a Netflix kind of documentawy special on Dad.'

'Have you told Dad?'

'No, we're too scared to. Dad kind of knows he's going for him no matter what. That's all he's talking about, and Towin would only get thwacked if he said as much. But it's twue, Decima. If it goes ahead, Daddy will get thwown in jail for taxes at least, never mind the west of it.'

'And?'

'Oh stop being so MEAN Decima. You know Daddy loves you, twuly loves you.'

I roll my eyes.

'He weally twied to make you love him, Decima. You wouldn't give him a chance. Anyway, you've GOT to stop this Twitter wubbish. It's not helping at all.'

As if I could.

As if I could start loving him, out of the blue. It's true, he and Petrina did throw every cliché in the book at us to make us love them. Robert the pony and the pair of chipmunks nearly won me over, they were my soulmates growing up, but you can't buy love. Nobody can. And I don't care what anybody says to the contrary, no matter how much they spoiled us, they couldn't replace our real parents. Well, not for me, they couldn't. They got Ornella at least. Hook, line and sinker.

'Trying to put the blame on me, I get it.' I glare at the ceiling.

'Oh, and by the way…'

She does this, I wait for it.

'What's with your shows lately?'

'What's with what? I didn't know you watched.'

'Daddy makes me… I thought you were supposed to be a witch?'

'Yes, the show, in case you forgot, is called *The Witch's Hour.*'

'I know that. But you don't come acwoss at ALL witchy.'

I hold my phone away from my ear.

'Don't you start.'

'It's all you flirting with the guests isn't it? What's witchy about that?'

'It's what the viewers want, Ornella. That's why they watch me.'

'Anyway. Daddy says you must do something to fix it. Be more witch, Deccy. Pwove it. Be more witch.'

'And screw you too,' I click off.

My thoughts return to that time with Scorpio. What if it's Lorelei? Sending spells to interrupt my interviews?

22

My family

Alice

Ha ha! I was taking a shower yesterday evening when I felt something touch my foot. I shrieked, got shampoo in my eyes and mouth and almost slipped over. I grabbed a towel to wipe my face, and when I looked down there was Zylch, covered in soapy bubbles and trying to catch the water in his paws. I never know what he'll get up to next. He's impossibly cute.

Jai hasn't contacted me for almost three weeks. All I do on Friday evenings and Saturday mornings is check my phone and look to see if he's downstairs outside the apartment.

By 11.00 am today, I accept he isn't coming, so I go to visit my parents. At least my mother's cooking will make me feel a bit better for a while.

Now that he's thriving it's time to return Zylch to my mother, although I'll miss this little guy. He rides along in my backpack. When I hop off the train, I take him out to sit on my shoulder while I walk briskly through the desolate landscape. We pass the Harding's old timber house. The windows are boarded up and there's a 'Sold' sign at the gate. They've lived here for more than forty years, and I'm surprised to see they've gone after all the work they put into the yard. I suppose old age caught up with them. Half a mile further on, the Dupont's place is also sold. Strange. The Brent Flats area has always attracted the hippy types and oddballs like my parents, and people don't usually move away once they've settled here. It's too bleak and unattractive for the townsfolk. Two houses sold? What's going on?

I was born and lived here most of my life. It's not for everyone. You have to truly appreciate nature and tranquility. No shops, no street lighting, no public transport. No hard roads. But – clean air, birdsong, fragrance of shrubs and wild plants, no traffic noise.

By the time I pass the Herrold place and see it's also sold, I know for sure something isn't right.

My father Patrick is already eating lunch by the time I arrive. His mealtimes never vary: breakfast at 7.30 am before he leaves for work. Lunch at 1.00 pm every day, whether at work or home. Dinner, on the dot of 7.00 pm. Everything has to be precise.

'Hi Dad,' I say. He glances up, nods briefly and continues eating. He looks tired.

My mother reheats my meal in the microwave, and while I eat she inspects Zylch.

'You've done well, Alice. I didn't think it would survive. Strange how it isn't mottled, although the silver coat is very pretty. It must have reverted.'

Astrid spent ten years cross breeding Screechers to get the unique mottled black and silver coat which she patented. Because they are so unique, Mottled Screechers command fifty times the price of a Common Screecher.

'But it's never going to be of any use to me. There's no anger in it. It's docile, soft. It would never make a fighter. I think the best thing would be to turn it out and see if it survives.'

I should be past being shocked by Astrid's approach to the Mottled Screechers. She breeds them to fight, to rip each other to pieces. If they don't, nobody will buy them, and she needs the money, particularly the money from the *Salvheal* oil. This old house is a money pit. What my father earns doesn't go far enough to maintain it. I feel a flush of anger rising from my neck up to my hairline. How can she be so callous, looking at this little silver kitten-like creature?

'I'll keep him,' I snap, taking him from her and tucking him against my neck.

My father has finished eating and moves his plate away. He sits staring at the table while my mother removes his plate.

'Are you OK, Dad?' I ask.

He looks at me blankly, as if he's never seen me before, then gives a little shake of his head and replies:

'Thank you, Alice. I'm perfectly well.'

He pushes away from the table and walks out of the room.

My mother is wiping the dishes.

'Can I talk to you please?' I ask.

She turns towards me, a plate and cloth in her hand, and blinks.

'Please. So many strange things seem to be going on. I'm worried, I don't know what to do, and I need somebody to talk to. I don't have anybody else.'

'Come on,' she says. 'It's feeding time. We can talk down there.'

I leave Zylch in my backpack and follow my mother down to the basement. The Mottled Screechers are restless, snarling, scratching at the glass, snapping at each other. Horrible things.

Astrid hauls a leg of beef from the chill room and feeds it into the pen. The creatures fall on it, devour it in seconds, leaving no sign it was ever there, then slink away to their lairs to sleep.

'Well, what is it?'

'Father. He doesn't look well. Is something wrong?'

'Nothing for you to worry about. He's fine, just a little tired. He has things on his mind. It doesn't need to concern you.'

'Why are all the other properties on the Flats sold? Why is everybody leaving? What's going on?'

She sighs. 'Alice, you know, things change. People change, circumstances change. I believe the Hardings had been wanting to move into town for a long time. The place became too much for them. I don't know about the others, but anyway, that's their business. Not ours.'

Why do I get the feeling she is holding something back?

She brushes her hands and turns towards the door.

'Astrid. There's something else I need to talk about.'

'Tell me.'

'I've met somebody I really like.'

'Good, dear, I'm pleased for you.'

I tell her about Jai. How he's polite and kind and friendly. How he obviously enjoys my company, but how he's never even held my hand. I tell her I am afraid to make the first move in case I frighten him away, but how I am beginning to feel I can't live without him. How I can't stop thinking about him. What should I do?

She listens silently, nodding occasionally. When I've finished, she says: 'Alice, you have the answer in your hands. You can use your power to achieve anything you wish. But be careful. This man is from a different culture to ours. It sounds as if you know almost nothing about him and you could end up badly hurt. You may be reading too much into this friendship. He is obviously lonely and enjoys having somebody like you to keep him company, but he will return to his own country one day. I think you would be unwise to expect too much.'

I agree with what she says, but it cannot change the way I feel about Jai. I DO have the power to make him love me. I could pull out one of the love spells, but I would never use it. It has to come freely from him.

Let me tell you about my mother, Astrid. The Nordic name suggests slender, long-haired blondes with dazzling toothy smiles and healthy tans. Witches are traditionally imagined to be skinny with lank black hair, a hooked nose and warty chin, wearing a pointy hat and black cloak. My mother doesn't look in any way Nordic, nor does she look in any way like a witch. She's short and plump with frizzy hair and a little button nose. She wears small gold-framed glasses. If you saw her pushing her trolley around the stores, you wouldn't give her a second glance.

That's what makes her so powerful, and dangerous when she needs to be. Nobody looking at her could ever guess she's a witch unless they looked into her eyes, when they'd see they are strangely ice blue, like the cold heart of a diamond.

Her powers have passed down through the female line since the beginning of time. Some have abused them, while others like me have hardly used them. In deference to my father, because he's uncomfortable with the magic thing, Astrid generally only uses them when it's absolutely necessary, although she throws a few simple spells to keep her hand in. Magic is like any other art. If you don't use it, you lose it, and you never know when it may be needed.

Screecher breeding has been a family business for generations. Over time the bloodlines had become weak from inbreeding, and Astrid was determined to produce a new strain that would not only be healthier and more aggressive, but also more beautiful. She took degrees in microbiology and genetic sequencing in order to produce a perfect Screecher in appearance and behavior.

My father is her soulmate. They adore each other. Unlike my mother, he is not a witch. He doesn't have any magical powers unless you count his engineering skills, which are pretty neat. He designed and built the entire Screecher breeding facility under the house. He is a bit of an ostrich where the magic is concerned. He turns a blind eye and he and Astrid have a tacit agreement that she will never do anything to embarrass him.

Before I leave, I'm surprised when Astrid says: 'Bring your young man for lunch one Sunday, if you like.'

I think about it for a moment.

'But you won't let him see any…'

'No. We'll be a 'normal' family,' she says. 'No abracadabra hocus-pocus.' She even smiles.

I tuck Zylch down my cleavage and sling the backpack onto my shoulder.

'I'll let you know about lunch,' I say.

When I look back, I see my father standing at an upstairs window, gazing out into space. I raise my hand and wave, but I don't think he notices me.

23

The oldest threat in the book

Decima

Newman and Gigg Brothers department store with its parquet floors and rattling old elevators is a time warp that creeps me out. I wouldn't normally be seen dead in the place, but needs must.

'What do you think?' I ask the girl, twisting my head right and left, up and down.

She nods approvingly.

Fake nod. I glare at her in the mirror. I haven't tried a reverse hair dip before. Purple streaks fade into black and trickle over my boobs to my waist. Maybe she could have done more with the extensions, made them go further down to my crotch. But it is what it is now. Instagram waits for nobody.

'Get me an exact matching purple eye shade and go heavy and long on the lashes.'

She sets to work. 'Going somewhere special?'

'I'm always going somewhere special,' I say with a finality that shuts her up.

I don't do small talk but, on the other hand, I like the murmur of her voice in my ear. I instruct her to keep talking. Which gets the girl all tongue-tied. It's clear she knows who I am and why I'm here. We're going through the motions.

The nerves are kicking in. I can't get this wrong and I take my time. It helps that she wears a name tag. Actually, I'm liking the buzz of the place, the passing stares, the glassy reflections and the heady perfume smells. Stop making excuses, and get on with it.

'So…' I exaggerate a look at her badge. 'Janita Tillman. What relation are you to the up-and-coming young journo?'

Her eyes harden.

'I know who you are,' she says.

'Then you know why I'm asking.'

She's wearing a cute little white denim dress. I look at her legs. 'Such pretty knees you have,' I say, turning away, tucking my chin in and muttering, 'Such a shame.'

That's it. Done.

She twists her mouth to one side.

Message received.

Oldest trick in the book. If your threats fall on deaf ears, take them to the family. I get no kick at all out of doing this but, like most threats, at least it's an empty one. A few words. Nothing more. Kneecapping is not my game. Or Dad's. It will keep him off my back, though, next time he calls, and, who knows, Rex Tillman might pull back a little. She's itching now to call her brother. So I spin it out.

'Would you mind doing me a few shots?'

I hand over my phone and get into pose. Holding onto my knees, first one, then the other, I gaze down at them fondly.

I'm satisfied with the result. She's good at getting the best Insta filters I tell her, and she's so pleased we chit chat for a while, as if what's been said had never been said.

'Enjoy your evening,' she calls as I leave the store.

I'm not going anywhere special tonight, but I have got two of the boys coming over later. I guess if I'm honest with myself, this is me making an effort. I'm sensing stuff. And it's not good. Alice is becoming quite the Little Miss Unobtainable Innocence, and they're lapping it up.

24

I'm walking on sunshine

Alice

I'm walking on sunshine, yay yay! The words of the old song spin through my head.

When I get home from my parents, Jai is waiting outside. Seems he was delayed on his way this morning. I say I hope he hasn't been waiting too long, but he replies he's only just got here. Must have been telepathy!

We take a walk around the park for half an hour. He's a little hesitant at first when I ask him to come to my parents' for lunch. I'm surprised when he tells me he doesn't eat meat – I thought all men did.

'In our family none of us eat meat. Many Sikhs don't. Our religion doesn't say we mustn't, but we prefer not to.'

'I don't either,' I say, 'my mother never cooks meat when I visit.' I gave up eating meat when I was eight and first saw the Mottled Screechers attacking a carcass.

'Please do come,' I continue. 'I think you'd like my folks, and they'd be so interested to hear about your background and your work.'

I nag him until he gives a little laugh and agrees.

This week has really dragged, although I've been busier than ever. Decima kept me going up and down, running unimportant errands downtown that one of the juniors could easily have done, but she seemed determined to keep me out of the Tower as much as possible. Strange, as usually she enjoys watching every move I make so that she can find something to complain about. Anyway, wherever I went and whatever I was doing, I was thinking of Jai all the time, counting the days and hours.

On Sunday I leave Zylch at home with a chunk of Parmesan and a peanut butter and jelly sandwich to keep him happy. I know this may sound silly, but I've started using Alexa to entertain him when I'm out for a long time. Random stuff, but I hope it keeps him from getting too bored or lonely, having something to listen to. He'll eat until his tummy is full, then he'll curl up on a cushion and sleep.

My heart thumps as I skip down the stairs to where Jai is waiting. I'm always shaky before meeting him, but the moment I see him and he smiles I feel completely relaxed. He's so easy to be with.

We travel by train and then walk the rest of the way. Jai doesn't mind the cooler weather. He says it gets cold in the winter in the Punjab where he comes from.

He's pleased that our house is on the Brent Flats, which is one area he is researching for his work. He takes a load of photos and some plant samples, but he's very quiet, I think probably nervous at the thought of meeting my family.

It's amazing. He gives Astrid a little wind chime made from dried seeds, which whispers when the breeze catches it. He and Patrick get on right away. I haven't seen my father so animated for years. He takes Jai to his studio and shows him his paintings and sculptures. It turns out Jai likes to paint too. He's never mentioned that to me.

My mother has excelled herself and produces a faultless meal. Jai compliments her and eats a second helping. While my father takes him for a walk around the property, I help Astrid with the dishes.

She says: 'Alice, he certainly is a charming young man and I can see he's very fond of you. We would love to see you settled down.'

Although they never said anything, and were always polite to Rory, I could tell they didn't take to him.

My heart blips. 'You really think so? I can't tell.'

'Yes, the aura tells me he cares for you deeply.'

My mother has never misread an aura.

He cares for me deeply. Nothing else matters. 'Is it going to last? Are we going to be together?'

'I can't see into the future, Alice. But I'm sensing great happiness and terrible pain.'

All I hear is 'He cares for you deeply.'

I give my mother a huge spontaneous hug, which alarms her. She pats me on the back and says: 'There, there.'

When we leave, I look back to see my father and mother both standing at the gate, waving.

Walking back to the station, I notice the Harding's house has been demolished.

I'm about to tell Jai that I'm worried that all the houses on the Brent Flats have been sold, but I don't want to spoil the magic of today. I walk very close to him, hoping he'll take my hand, but his hands are in his pockets, so instead I hook my arm through his. He doesn't resist. Knowing now how much he cares for me, I'm happy to take things slowly. It's probably a cultural thing, that you don't rush into a relationship. You take your time.

I am SO, SO happy I could weep.

He sees me to my apartment, and I pluck up the courage to invite him in for a coffee. 'Or *chai*, if you like – I've been practicing making it!'

Jai looks into my eyes and I catch a flash of sadness before he gives a little smile and says: 'I've enjoyed our day together Alice. I really have. I'll see you again soon.'

I watch him walk away, hoping he'll turn and wave, but he doesn't look back. The sunshine fades out of me.

Then I remind myself – he does care for me. He'll see me again soon. A glimmer of sunshine leaks back in.

When I open the door, Zylch runs to me, stretching up his arms and squeaking. I hold his soft, silky body against my neck and whisper: 'It's going to be OK, Zylch. He loves me.'

Now that I'm certain, I call Shelley to tell her about Jai.

After speaking to her I'm feeling a bit deflated. She says she's happy for me, but worried that Jai is from a different culture which could cause problems between us.

Why would anybody think that people from different cultures can't be in love?

25

Seriously strange

Ramon

Decima always has a surprise up her sleeve. You never know what she's going to demand, but whatever it is, you obey if you want to keep your job. I thought that I'd seen everything in the last couple of years I've been working here, but what happened on Saturday night is so far from anything I could have imagined, I'm still in shock.

She called me up to her office on Friday morning and took me straight through to the Passion Pit.

'You know what to do,' she said. 'Get on with it.'

When we'd finished, she rolled away from me, climbing off the bed and sliding into her bath.

I walked over and looked down at her. 'How was that?' I asked.

She stared up at me.

'Efficient as ever. Now get lost.'

I got dressed and turned to leave, when she called out: 'Ramon. Are you doing anything Saturday evening?'

'Ah, I don't work Saturdays, Decima.'

'It's not work. It's social. I'd like to invite you to my home.'

That stopped me in my tracks.

'Say again?'

'Come and spend an evening with me on Saturday. Tell Cory I'd like him to come too.'

What was she planning?

Back in the basement, I drew a couple cups of coffee and took one over to Cory.

'Hey man, you free Saturday evening?'

'Depends what for.'

'Decima. Her place. She's invited the two of us.'

He tapped his mouth with a finger and pulled his bottom lip down, then said: 'Why not? Any idea what she's thinking?'

'Nope. No idea. Who knows what goes on in her mind.'

'Yes, OK, I'm up for it. We can ride together in the Beetle.'

We reach Decima's house at 7.30. Takes a while to get through all the security. She welcomes us like old friends and leads us to her living room. She's barefoot, wearing a soft wool outfit, with her hair loose over her shoulders. She's coloured it in horrible black and purple streaks and looks like a small kid wearing a too big wig, kind of Halloweenish. Without her power clothes, harsh make-up and shoes, she looks small and innocent. She smells of soap and shampoo.

I was expecting her house to be modern, stainless steel, glass, minimalist, but it's the exact opposite. There are big soft armchairs and sofas, a thick carpet, wood paneled walls and an open fireplace. There's a whiff of woodsmoke, vases of flowers. One entire wall is occupied by shelves filled with books.

'Thanks for coming guys. Make yourselves at home, be comfortable. What can I get you to drink? Wine, beer, something else?' She's playing the perfect hostess.

Sitting opposite each other, sipping our beers, I sense that Cory is feeling as puzzled as I am. This isn't what we were expecting. Decima chats about her show, about the latest films, about our hobbies. For the first time since I met her, I can actually feel myself liking her.

We sit there for an hour, relaxed, having a couple more beers. Decima is charming and funny. I'm waiting for her next move.

She goes and sits next to Cory, curling up her feet on the sofa and resting her head on his shoulder, laughing as she remembers when Kirk Douglas was a guest on her show and tripped over the step onto the platform. 'He was an old guy, but boy did he still have something special,' she smiles. I notice her hand gently stroking Cory's thigh. She's touching him, but she's looking at me, her eyes glittering, running her tongue over her lips and smiling.

I go and sit beside her and put my arm over her shoulder. She gives a little sigh, and says:

'Come on guys, let's go to bed.'

We follow her to her bedroom, which like the living room is colorful and cozy, with books piled on the table beside the bed.

'What shall we have for starters?' she asks as we strip off and climb onto the bed.

Cory and I make a good team. We know what she likes and we know how to supply it.

Afterwards we all lie in a tangled heap.

'You naughty, naughty boyth.' Decima says in a funny little girl voice. 'You detherve a good thmacking.'

'Mmm, yes please,' Cory chuckles.

'We'll all have a nithe thyower, and then we'll thtart again!'

When it's all over, Cory starts dressing, but Decima says 'Come back to bed, Cory. You too Ramon. Come and lie down.'

Cory's face is a picture of dismay. We've both given as much as we can for one night.

Decima laughs. 'It's OK, it's time to sleep now.'

Tentatively we climb back into bed, one on each side of her, waiting for her next move.

She gives a small smile, closes her eyes and reaches over to the bedside lights, clicking them off. 'Goodnight,' she says. Five minutes later she's snuggled up to Cory, gently snoring through her large nose. I move close and put my arm around her.

Cory is soon asleep too, but I lie awake wondering

what this is all about. It's so out of character for Decima.

A cool breeze flutters the curtains, and I carefully pull a cover from the foot of the bed over the three of us.

Sometime during the night, I wake. In the light from the moon where it slips through the curtains, I glance at Decima's face, and see a small tear on her cheek. I stroke it off with my thumb. She reaches out for my hand, but I'm not sure if she's asleep or awake.

I wake in the morning as Cory comes out from the shower. There's no sign of Decima, so we follow the aroma of coffee and find a table on the shaded terrace, with a pot of coffee, a plate of pastries and a jug of juice. There's a note propped up against the coffee pot. 'Help yourselves boys.'

We eat and drink in silence and sit facing the sun, relaxing with our eyes closed.

A voice comes from behind the terrace.

'What a beautiful girl you are, Decima. I do love you. You are the very, very best. My little beauty. My kind, sweet girl. I love you, darling girl. Cutest girl in the whole world. Little Miss Loveliness. My darling.'

Cory looks at me and crooks an eyebrow. It sounds like Decima talking to herself.

We tiptoe to the edge of the terrace and peer around the corner.

Beneath a vine-covered pergola, sitting in a large, gilded cage, a white cockatoo stares at us with black beady eyes, and says in perfect imitation of Decima's voice:

'What a beautiful girl you are, Decima. I do love you. Little Miss Loveliness. Trevor's little darling.'

The bird climbs onto a swing and rocks back and forwards, whistling. 'Oh my darling, oh my darling, oh my darling Decima…'

'Why in the name of holy kamoley are you still here!' screeches our hostess. She's shiny with sweat and dressed for running, with a headband holding her hair off her enraged, screwed-up face.

Cory and I turn and stare open-mouthed, as she stamps her foot and waves her hand. 'Go on. Out! This isn't a bloody hotel. And by the way – anything that goes on here, here stays here! Keep your mouths closed if you want to keep your jobs.'

We walk silently back to the car.

'She's bonkers, isn't she?' says Cory. '101% nuts. What the heck was that? She's taught a bird to tell her she's wonderful?'

'Seriously strange bro. Seriously strange.'

And now it's Monday, a new week begins at The Tower, and Decima is as much of a bitch as ever, looking at us like we're dirt she scraped off her shoe.

26

Dinner date

Alice

It's happening. Jai is taking me out to dinner for the first time. He says he has something important to tell me.

There is nothing in my wardrobe for a special occasion, and I want to look beautiful for him, so I've bought myself a gorgeous outfit. To be honest I've never been any good at choosing clothes, so I asked the salesgirl at Glam to pick something out. Because I'm what she described as 'statuesque' and could wear something big and bold, she chose a stunning gypsy dress in sapphire blue with a ruby red bodice and a kind of red scarf edged with dangling golden coins that drapes over my hips. The blouse is off the shoulder, and the full skirt sways and swings as I walk. I'd never have dared even try something so flamboyant, but I feel fabulous. Looking in the mirror I barely recognise myself. The dress emphasizes all my curves and brings out the blue of my eyes. She adds some sparkly drop earrings that tinkle when I turn my head, a dozen golden bangles and red strappy high-heeled sandals.

When I tell her it's for a special occasion, she takes me to the beauty department and books me in for a full treatment – pedicure, manicure, facial, make-up and hair styling.

'Have you thought about a fragrance?' she asks, steering me to the perfume counter.

Shelley gave me a bottle of perfume last Christmas, but Decima made a comment about 'the ghastly smell of your cheap scent,' so I'd stopped wearing it.

'Is there something that smells of coconut and spices?' I ask.

The salesgirl smiles and wipes a tiny swab on my wrist.

'Try this. Tom Ford's Private Blend Soleil Blanc. Very coconutty.'

Ooh. I close my eyes and inhale the scent. It's rich but dainty, clean and exotic, and exactly right.

I see myself sitting in the sunshine, beside Jai, on a tropical beach, listening to the waves lapping and the birds singing, feeling a warm breeze. 'I'll take it,' I say.

She wraps it delicately and hands it to me in a tiny golden bag. I gulp when I see the price. It's a very small bottle. I've spent a month's salary in the last hour, but I don't care because I feel like a million dollars and I am going to make Jai so, so proud of me.

I take the afternoon off work on Friday to go for my beauty treatment. When I walk out my skin is glowing, my finger and toenails polished to perfection, my hair falling in soft waves around my shoulders. I know I look beautiful, although I don't really look like myself.

Feeling sick with nerves, and shaking with excitement, I dress carefully, check my make-up and dab Soleil Blanc behind my ears and on my wrists. From the mirror, a voluptuous confident woman gazes back at me.

Jai has booked a cab to take me to the restaurant. The driver looks at me admiringly and gives a little whistle. We pull up at a small restaurant a little out of town. The cab driver holds open the door. As I climb from the cab my knees tremble. I swallow, put my shoulders back and step into the restaurant.

The *maitre d'* greets me with a bow. 'Miss Archer? Please follow me.'

All eyes turn to watch as we weave through the tables into the far corner where Jai is waiting. He stands up as he sees us approaching. I'm welling up with happiness, feeling like a bride walking down the aisle to meet her groom. He looks into my eyes, his expression very serious.

As the *maitre d'* pulls out a chair and eases me into it a waiter brings the menus. Jai and I haven't spoken, just looked at each other silently.

I stare blankly at the menu. I don't know anything about fancy food, so I ask Jai to order for me.

He speaks to the waiter and lays the menu down.

I glance around and notice all the other diners are

casually dressed.

I realize I am out of place and must look foolish.

'You look very, very beautiful, Alice,' says Jai quietly.

I smile ruefully. 'I think I've overdone it.'

Years from now, if you ask me, I will not be able to tell you what the waiter placed in front of us. All I will remember is staring at the plate and feeling the thumping of my heart.

Jai is even quieter than usual. There's none of our usual banter and I realize he too is conscious of the importance of the occasion. We are thinking of our future.

I push away my empty plate and smile at him.

For the first time since we met, he takes my hand in his long brown fingers, the skin so smooth and warm, the nails so polished.

'Alice. I think you know how much our friendship means to me.'

I nod.

'Meeting you is the best thing that's happened to me since I came to America. You bring so much fun and pleasure to my life.'

My stomach is turning cartwheels, waiting for what he will say next.

'There's something I need to explain to you. In my culture, family is of extreme importance. There are laws we live by, rules that we must obey. As I told you once, it can be very restrictive, which is the reason I came here, to try to find myself and what I want from life. To escape the ties of obligation.'

I nod.

He sighs and I feel a small shiver down my spine.

'Alice. Oh Alice. Not for anything would I hurt you. You have become so precious to me.'

I feel slightly sick.

'I am returning to India for six months.'

I relax. I can wait six months. I will wait six months. Six years. I will wait however long it takes.

I smile brightly. 'It's fine, Jai. I know you must have things to do there and to see your family. I'll wait.'

Jai says: 'I'm going to be married.'

A small croak bursts out from my throat. The world tilts and I feel tears building up behind my eyes.

I manage to smile and nod, saying I am going to the washroom and will be back in a few minutes.

I stand up and walk calmly towards the washroom. When I am out of sight I stumble out of the restaurant and wave down a cab.

As it pulls away, I hear Jai shouting my name. I don't look back. It feels as if my heart has been ripped from my body. I pay the cab driver and stagger up to my apartment as the tears begin to flow.

I kick off my shoes and fall down onto the floor, screaming into my arm, scratching at my face, tearing at my hair, kicking my bare feet against the floorboards. I dig my teeth into my arm and bite until I taste blood.

I hear the entrance door swing open, footsteps running up the stairs, then Jai's voice calling me as he bangs on the door of my apartment.

'Alice, please let me in. Let me talk to you.'

I lie on the floor, rocking, weeping, hurting myself.

I ignore Jai until he finally gives up, and his footsteps fade away. Then I sob and sob until I fall asleep.

When the morning light creeps through the window, I'm still lying on the floor. Zylch has snuggled up to me and is stroking me with his small pink fingers.

I drag myself up and undress, heaping the gypsy dress and the sandals and jewelry into a bundle that I shove down the garbage chute. I open the bottle of Soleil Blanc and empty it down the lavatory.

I curl up in bed, with Zylch beside me, and sleep again until dark. Then I shower, and hack off my hair, leaving ragged spikes.

My heart is shattered. It is hard, icily cold and filled with incandescent rage. Damn you Jai. Damn you. Why did you have to do this to me?

27

No two things are different

Decima

'OK, so what went on there?'

'What went on where?'

'Come on, it's the big question. You know, what happens when you die. Tell the world. We don't get real ghosts on the show very often.'

'When you die? Well, you don't die, do you? Nobody dies.'
'Really?'

'Every day you're living in the living, you're living in the dead.'
'What does that mean?'

'You, me, everybody, we're two souls, one is here in the world, the other waits around, ready to take over. Think of it like a lift. One of those funicular lifts. Or a ski lift. What goes down goes up… it's really all very simple… No two things are different. No two things are the same.'

'What, like the Yin and Yang?'

Oh shut up Miss Beach Mansion Million Dollar Cowface. I switch Lorelei's YouTube channel off in disgust and march to the window. It is too cold and windy

150

to go out onto the terrace but if I squeeze myself sideways with my face against the glass, I can look out to sea. The ocean is wild today, crashing around the rocks, and I can't help but think of the waves lapping at the sand by Lorelei's Malibu beach house. I torture myself with her Insta feed. Surrounded by gold, diamonds and boys, she stretches out on her sun deck, counting the dollars. Yes, boys. At her age too. She must be all of 50. How? However can I better that? First, I need details.

Josh was up on the studio floor the day of the ghost interview. I call him and order him to be at my Passion Pit early the next morning before anybody else is in.

I get up extra early to work on my look. I go for a Chanel meets dominatrix vibe. A stylish but killer pink woven wool mini dress with two great bows hitching it up at the thighs. Fine diamante straps match a jewel-encrusted dog-collar choker, its diamante lead clipped to a bracelet.

I'm getting the set ready for the afternoon's interview when he arrives. Keeping my back to him, I take Digby out of his Hermes bag and settle him on his shelf, giving him a little tickle on the stomach before wheeling around.

'What's this about?' He's got that smile going, a smile I know well. I glance down at his trousers. As I thought. Job done, thank you outfit.

I go straight in before my own mind starts to turn to other things. 'We need to up the ante on the interview.'

'What interview?'

'What interview he says,' I roll my eyes. '*That* interview. The GHOST interview. We need another viral show. Soon, and nothing half-baked.'

'What's the hurry?'

'The ratings, Josh. The whole Twitter storm rumors that I'm not a witch, that the whole show is fake, are growing. If we don't pull something out of the bag soon there'll be trouble. The sponsors won't renew their contact. I need to prove it.'

'Prove what?'

'That I'm a witch, stupid.'

'But you're not a witch.'

I give him a long hard stare.

He stares back. He glances over his shoulder and then back, like he'd run if he could.

'You're the special effects genius, Josh, not me. Come up with something. It's got to be the best show ever. It's got to make interviewing a real ghost look like an old rerun of some cheesy old *been there done that* talk show.'

He's still giving me the long hard look.

I stare him out.

He wins.

'What?'

'Decima.' An amused smile plays across his lips.

'WHAT?'

'Oh Decima, Decima.'

I stare blankly at him.

He comes towards me, puts an arm on my shoulder and looks me in the eyes. 'You know. We *all* know.'

'Know WHAT?'

'I hate to break it to you, Decima, but ghosts don't exist.'

'But! —'

The penny drops along with my jaw. I push past him and march away. Then back. I can't take this in.

'I'm not only the King of SEX, Decima, I'm the King of SFX remember. Special Effects genius right here.'

'You *duped* the whole thing? Wait…' I go to Digby's shelf and look into his brown button eyes. 'You hear that?!' I stand there with Digby for a moment whilst my brain catches up with what I'm hearing. I turn and stride halfway up to Josh, stopping dead in my tracks, hands on my hips. 'You duped *everyone*,' I shriek. 'The *world*?'

His smile says it all. I can barely breathe.

'Lorelei Thornheart, the Witch Queen of LA, is definitely not a real witch?'

'Fake as a five million dollar Bitcoin note.'

'I KNEW it, I knew it, I knew it.'

'That's not what you've been saying.'

'I know, I was taken in by the online rubbish. How could I have let myself be persuaded otherwise? She really, really is a fake. That's the last time I don't follow my instincts.'

This is news on so many levels. Whole religions have grown up around Lorelei Thornheart and her 'no two things are different, no two things are the same' riddle-setting ghost. The Two Souls Spiritualist Chapel in LA is trending on YouTube. My brain explodes. I scream. Then go very quiet. We're standing staring at each other, Josh's eyes glinting with amusement.

'Could we do it again?' I ask quietly.

'Now come on, you're no 2-bit copycat, Deccy.'

I ignore his abuse of my name.

'I don't mean *that*. But some kind of magic… *stuff* to, to show the audience that I'm a real witch too.'

Josh's shoulders are shaking. He's giggling. This is so unlike Josh. I've never seen him laughing before, he's a smiler, not a laugher.

'I hate to break it to you, Decima, but witches don't exist either.'

'Well, I know that!' I lie, I was never sure. 'But I've still got to, somehow, prove it or we're all finished.'

'Or?'

'Or what?'

He raises his eyebrows. 'Or we could expose her.'

For a second my heart soars, before crashing again. 'Don't be a fool. The whole station would be shut down for fraud.'

He's still laughing.

'Josh you're wicked,' I joke back, laughing.

The thought of Holier than Thou Witch Queen of LA Lorelei Thornheart crumbling to obscurity and probably prison for fraud takes a dangerous hold of my thoughts.

'It's a gorgeous idea, if it didn't mean that we would all crash down with her in a sea of lawsuits. Tower and all. OK, be serious now. I really need your help.'

He goes up to Digby, turns him to face the wall, spins round to me and stands there staring, legs astride like some great white blue-eyed bear.

'One good turn deserves another.' He puts his head to one side and beckons me with one finger.

I smile. It's kind of cute that we still turn each other on so much.

I slink over to him. 'I should have known asking you in here could only end one way.'

His hands are on my waist. They reach nearly all the way round. Everything, but everything, about Josh is big.

'Hey, big man,' I whisper. 'So you'll help me?'

He pulls me closer, 'Whaddaya think?'

His hands slip slowly down my back. 'Not now, Josh, I've got a show to prepare.'

'Remember, one good turn deserves another Deccy.'

'This is a SET Josh, the cameras might be on.'

'I hope they are,' he holds me tighter. I pull away.

We're both playacting, we know exactly where this is going.

'Digby, close your eyes.'

'He's looking the other way! But hey whatever you say,' he grabs my hand and makes for the bed. I pull him back, 'Not there. That's the set.'

I steer him to the boudoir powder puff chair and we're immediately all over each other.

As we're about to go all the way and become one, I pull away from him.

'NO, Decima. No teasing,' he pleads.

'Oh, one thing. While we're here, what is going on with you guys and that girl down in the basement?'

'Alice?' His eyes suddenly go very wide, as if he's remembered something. He lets out a loud groan and it's all over before it's begun.

'I'm sorry,' he gasps. 'You were teasing me.'

I roll off him onto the white Greek flokati rug. My elbow catches in the diamante lead, nearly choking me. I stay on my front, hiding my fuming face. I'll need to change my whole look and fast, but I manage to summon the actress in me and soften my eyes as I turn to look up at him.

'Hug me, Josh. Hug me for a moment, my big boy.' Stealthily I crawl up, cat-like, into his lap and wrap my legs around him.

He starts apologizing again.

'Shush sush now,' I put a finger over his mouth. Is there anything worse than a man saying he's sorry, out loud, in words, for not satisfying a woman?

'So you, too, then, clearly have got the hots for… for… that girl?'

'You know what, Deccy? There's nothing like a jealous woman to turn a man on. You teased me right at the wrong moment there. You got me going in seconds, you know that. Nobody can replace you. Alright, I'll be honest with you. Here's the thing. You know the real reason I wouldn't fess up to that fakery? Not for a million dollars? Life has never been so sweet. Where else am I gonna get a billion dollars worth of your style and class any time I want? And those boys. We're the crack team, you know that.'

Hmm. That's the best I'm going to get for now.

I snuggle into his chest. His hand rests on my cheek which he strokes over and over, ever so lightly, with his thumb. This is dangerous. Time is really ticking, I'm starting to tingle all over again and we're in a danger zone.

'Tell me, Josh, tell me now. The fake ghost. How did you do it?'

28

No sympathy

Alice

What a fool I was to imagine Jai could love me, that we would be together. How he must have laughed to himself when he saw me all dressed up like a gypsy queen. How could I have believed that I was beautiful?

After that evening, when he destroyed my dreams, I found a note pushed beneath my door. I knew what it would say, about how he didn't mean to upset me, how he wished me good luck and happiness, and thanking me for my friendship. I didn't need to read it. I screwed it up and tossed it across the room.

I want to cry. To stay curled up and cry myself away into nothing and nowhere.

I don't eat for four days. I, who have always thought of food first thing in the morning and all through the day. Who goes to bed thinking about what to eat the next day. Nothing tempts me. I feel weak and light-headed and sick, but the thought of food nauseates me.

I drag myself to work, ignoring strange looks and

enquiries if I'm OK. I'm immune to Decima's acid spite.

At home, Zylch watches me with sad eyes. He sits beside me, his little pointed chin resting on my foot and at night he lies on my pillow, breathing softly into my cropped hair. I pull him into my neck and weep into his silver fur. He waits patiently until I remember to feed him and sits at the window looking out as I leave for work. If I didn't have him to care for I'd run away, vanish.

A scrawny creature with ragged hair, dead eyes and a downturned mouth stares back lifelessly from the mirror. My clothes hang off me. At 25 I'm a haggard old woman. I've ignored calls from my mother and Shelley. I can't face telling them. Seeing the pity, listening to their platitudes and reminders of the 'cultural differences' they warned me about.

I'm slouched on the sofa, idly twiddling Zylch's coat, when the door buzzer goes. My heart leaps for a second – certain it's Jai. I run to the door and fling it open.

Shelley stands there, with her two little girls. I stare open-mouthed as she pushes past me into the apartment. She lifts Zylch off the sofa, puts him on the windowsill and sits the girls down with her phone, telling them to amuse themselves.

She takes me by the arm and pulls me into the kitchen, closing the door.

'I've been calling you for three days. I've been worried out of my mind. What's going on with you? '

Because of my silence she's made the difficult and

costly journey right across town with the children. I hang my head and mumble 'Sorry.'

'You look so rough,' she says, and folds me into her arms.

She listens while I sob on her shoulder, spilling out my misery until I'm empty.

I'm expecting sympathy, so it comes as a shock when she says: 'OK, I hear you. I feel your hurt, but I think you're overreacting. He didn't make you any promises. It sounds as if you misread it. He's doing what he believes is right. You can't blame him for that.'

She takes both my hands in hers. 'Alice, life goes on. You can't change what's done. Tearing yourself to pieces isn't doing you any good. Go and take a shower while I clean up the mess in here.' She puts her hands on my shoulders, turns me around and pushes me gently to the bathroom.

I hit the hot tap and stand in the stream, letting the water run down my body, rinsing away the stale smell, scalding my skin until it's pink and glowing. Then I run the cold, gasping and shivering from the shock. I rub myself dry and wrap myself in a clean toweling robe. I wipe the condensation from the mirror and look into my eyes. I see sadness there, but a hint of something else too. Resolve. I raise my chin.

Shelley has cleaned and tidied the kitchen and is sitting in the living room with Zylch on her lap. The girls are giggling over a game on her phone.

'Drink,' she smiles, handing me a mug.

I sit down next to her, sipping the coffee.

'Thank you, Shelley. That's what I needed. You're right; I was foolish. I'm OK now.'

'Cute little creature. I didn't know you had a cat. It is a cat, isn't it?'

'No,' I reply, absent-mindedly. 'It's a Screecher.'

She laughs. 'Ha ha, a Screecher. You're so funny.'

It's early evening and the light is fading from the sky. I call for a pizza delivery from Angeli's, and the four of us sit eating silently. I give Zylch pieces of crust, and Shelley laughs.

'I've never known a cat that eats pizza!' she says.

She glances at her watch. 'I'm off now. The girls have school tomorrow.' While she begins to collect her things and put the children's coats on, I call for a cab, ignoring her protests.

I hug them and wave them away, then I head out to the stores.

29

Questions

Decima

I dab at Josh's betrayal on my dress over and over. Google has told me that this kind of stain doesn't need dry cleaning. Dish soap and lukewarm water will do it.

This dress isn't real Chanel, but it's not far off. Way too expensive to throw in the bin. I really should hire more of my on-screen outfits from Sheenah. Leave her to deal with this stuff. Though not *this* particular stuff, news of it would be in every A, B and C lister's inbox before she could turn off the tap. *Nobody* can see this.

A big part of my fake witchy look are my Shellac, ruby-encrusted, purple talons. I got them taken off for the job in hand. Short nails make me feel like a scruff, but needs must.

I watch *Selling Sunset* on Netflix as I work, fixated on their immaculate hands. How long before Lorelei turns up on this show as one of their multi-million-dollar clients, manicured to within an inch of her life, looking for an upgrade on her beach house?

I'm a glutton for punishment. My mind is racing between the proof in my hands that my boys really have all lost their minds over that girl, and the bare-cheeked fakery of that witch Lorelei Thornheart. I *have* to trump her. But how? I go over what Josh said again and again, looking for an answer.

He said the ghost trick was a recording. But I'm still struggling to work out how they got away with it.

'So everybody knew?'

'Only me, Lorelei and the camera operators were in the studio that day. Closed set. All the crew were on a big bonus and had to sign NDAs. Any word getting out from one of them and they'd all be ruined and unemployable for the rest of their lives. Everyone knows ghosts are sensitive, right? He was only going to appear before Lorelei. So we pretended the live show was carrying on whilst the vision mixer down in the basement hit the play VT button at exactly the right second. Seamless, though I say so myself.'

'When did you film it? Who played the ghost?'

'Questions, questions.'

'Well, she owes you one. You're a decent man, Josh. You could truly clean up with that news. Retire yourself to Malibu.'

'I'm not sayin' I haven't thought about it. I'm a normal guy, right. But here's the thing, we all value our jobs, our *life*, here more.'

I don't believe that for a second. His own reputation

is what he means.

'If I came clean, there'd be plenty to build on away from Hawk Bay. Hollywood would be fighting for me and my SFX genius. Or London, or Bollywood, even. But I'm old enough to know this life we got here is *special*. It can't be replaced. And I'm meaning you, Decima. There isn't any other job like this in the world.' He touched my cheek with his fist and mock punched me.

I took it. I wish I could believe it.

Why? *Why* am I here at the sink washing a soiled dress that's way too young for me, even with my figure? It's me who should be in LA, where I belong. Way more than Josh. Way more than Lorelei Lieface. All I needed was the break. I can act. I'm a brilliant actor. A part in some low-key series would have done, would have given me the work and the independence I always craved. Instead that deceitful witch is living MY life. All of it based on a lie. A barefaced lie.

I don't know what's more annoying. Josh's evidence right in my hands, Alice's unconcerned *Innocence of the Unavailable* or Lorelei Thornheart doing over Dad and Josh as a stepping-stone to her own sea view golden bathtub.

What if Josh did call her out? She'd be ruined, but then so would we. My show would finish. The whole of CGO TV would collapse under legal challenges. But then? Supposing? What if CGO TV doesn't last anyway, with that documentary threat, and all of Dad's tax problems going on. Then what? Could Josh, the boys and I leave and start over? What was he saying about Bollywood, or London? Or San Antonio even? I've heard San Antonio is the place to be. But then Dad would cut me off, if he wasn't ruined himself by then. The only thing that is guaranteed to last is the boys' infatuation with Alice. That isn't going anywhere. My #1 task in all this is to, somehow, stop them lusting after her.

And then the idea comes to me. All of it. All at once. In a flash. I know exactly what to do.

As for Lorelei, something Josh said earlier is echoing over and over in my mind. I've got it, I've got the show. And it's genius.

I turn off the faucet and throw the dress in the trash.

30

Unsettled

Alice

Since I've started jogging to and from work, I've dropped two sizes. It left me a bit puffed the first few days, but it's getting easier. The security guy at the Tower called out this morning:

'Hey, loving the punk hair – it really suits you. Looking a million dollars Alice!'

Decima did a double-take the first day I turned up in camo trousers and a vest top, the clip-on nose ring and ear cuffs. For once she was lost for words; the best she could do was a little sneer.

'Fancy dress party?'

So you see, I'm really trying to get myself together. Even if inside I'm still broken, I'm not letting anybody see. I don't want pity.

Sean was waiting outside when I jogged home yesterday. He asked if I minded if he jogged with me. I couldn't say no – it's a public park. But – for heaven's sake – he was actually waiting outside my apartment this morning. As soon as I saw him, I backtracked and **_Broomsticked_** to work from the window. He arrived at work an hour later and gave me a funny look.

I hope he's not going to become a stalker.

I think I'm starting to get over Jai, until I see his photo in the Morning Herald. On the 3rd page.

'Jai Mahan, our Senior Research Coordinator, has taken a six-month sabbatical and returned to his homeland to wed his fianceé, Miss Jasminder Kaur. The marriage takes place next month in Amritsar. Jai's colleagues wish him every happiness and look forward to his return.'

My stomach turns itself inside out. I feel I'm going to vomit. I'm not over him, I'll never be over him. I realize I read too much into our friendship, as Shelley said, but to me he will always be the one. There will never be anyone else.

I curl up in a chair and stare out of the window as the words go around in my head: 'to wed his fiancée'. So he knew he was engaged when he was seeing me. I don't know which is worse, the pain or the anger.

Zylch gives a small squeak. He's sitting on the windowsill, and when he sees me look at him, he does a little jump, turns head over heels and lands on the rug. He jumps back up to the windowsill and does the same, turning his head to see if I'm watching. I can't help a grin. He runs around in a circle, lies on his back clutching his tail and humming. All the time his eyes are on me.

'Well done, Zylch,' I say. He hops over to the chair and bounces up onto my lap, staring up into my eyes. He reaches out and pushes up my lips at the corners, so I'm smiling at him. Then he tucks his head under my chin and taps gently on my neck as if he's telling me: 'Don't forget. I'm here.'

I hold him in my hands and press my face into his shiny pelt, leaning back in the chair with my eyes closed.

When I awake, I go to the kitchen and switch on the coffee machine, placing Zylch on the worktop. He sits watching, reaching out to touch the mug and withdrawing his finger with a noise that sounds like 'Ouch!'

'Yes Zylch, it's hot,' I say, turning to go back to my chair.

'Hot,' says a voice behind me.

I stop in my tracks and turn round, open mouthed.

'Zylch, did you *speak*?'

He stares back at me, and *winks*.

I call my mother. She sounds breathless when she answers.

'Can Screechers speak?' I ask.

'What an extraordinary question! Of course they can't speak, Alice. They're animals.'

'You're absolutely sure?'

'Yes, Alice,' she says with audible patience, 'they don't talk. How is your young man?'

Keeping my voice level, as I don't want her to know I'm hurting, I say brightly, 'He's back in India at the moment. Gone to visit family.'

I change the subject quickly. 'How's Father? He looked tired when I saw you last.'

'He's fine. We're both fine. I'll call you when we're not so busy. Take care.'

I'm about to ask if she's OK, when she hangs up.

My mother has never been too busy to talk. Even when we don't see each other for weeks, we have always had time for chats. She wants to get me off the line. Something doesn't feel right. We're not one of those families who spend all our time together, the way some families do, but if anything is wrong, we unite. I'm going to go and see them and find out what's going on.

I'm sitting pondering this when I remember the reason I called Astrid.

Zylch is wandering around in the kitchen, playing with the cupboard handles.

I try an experiment.

'Zylch, come here.'

He scampers in and sits by my feet, looking up with what seems to be a smile on his face.

'You understand, don't you? You actually understand what I say. And you can talk. Or am I hallucinating?'

As I sip my hot coffee, Zylch makes a slurping noise, and then giggles. He's definitely giggling.

You know what? I'm worried about my parents, broken by the man I love, and now I'm hallucinating, thinking I have a talking Screecher. I say, 'I'm going to bed, Zylch.'

He hops ahead of me to the bedroom and climbs on the bed beside my pillow. I slide under the comforter and pull him into me, like a teddy bear. 'Goodnight, Zylch', I say.

'Goodnight Alice'.

I fall asleep to the pulse of his heart.

31

Confiding

Alice

It's a bright but chilly Saturday. I pull on a jacket and put Zylch in my backpack, telling him to stay out of sight. He nods, and I'm pretty certain he understands everything I say.

I walk down to the harbor and sit on a bench against a wall, my eyes closed, thinking. I need to know what is happening with my parents so I can try to find a way to help them. What is going on with them? Is it a health problem? Financial? No, I'm sure it can't be. My mother would have told me, I know. What then? Divorce? Oh for goodness sake Alice, give your head a wobble. They are, always have been and always will be the most devoted couple. Nothing could come between them. It's something else. Why won't Astrid tell me? That is really worrying me.

Another thing is, I've realized that keeping Zylch in a small apartment isn't right. He needs outside space, somewhere to run. I don't know how I'm going to be able to afford to live anywhere that will give him the safe and happy environment he needs.

Those words 'to wed his fiancée' keep turning in my mind, stabbing me in the heart.

I'm lost in my thoughts, when a shadow falls over my face, blocking out the sun.

'*Hola*! What's a pretty girl doing sitting here on her own?'

I look up to see Josh grinning down at me.

'Would the lady mind if I shared her bench?' he asks.

'Sure,' I reply, putting the backpack down on the ground and moving over to make room for him.

Of the four, Josh is my favorite. He's a lot older than the others, maybe that's why I feel most comfortable with him. He's really attractive, with thick gray hair, bronze tan, bright blue eyes and a kind smile. Plus that seductive Texan drawl.

He sits quietly for a few minutes, and then asks: 'So what brings you down to the harbor?'

'Well, I like the activity. Getting out into the fresh air. Normal people doing normal things. It clears my head after a week in The Tower.'

'I get it. We surely do need some decompression time. Working for Decima ain't for the faint-hearted and fragile. I've always been curious about why you work for her. The way she treats you. There are plenty of other opportunities for a girl like you. Why do you put up with it? Is it the money?'

I shrug. 'Actually, I really love my job. It's close to where I live and I do get to meet interesting people, you know. I guess I could look for something else; maybe I'm too lazy. I won't be there forever. I'm fascinated by Decima, why she's the way she is. She seems to have everything, but sometimes I feel she has nothing.'

Josh stands up and walks away, coming back with a couple of coffees, handing one to me.

'I hear you. So, tell me, what about you? You have family around here?'

'They live out on the Brent Flats. My father's an engineer. My mother stays at home. We're a very ordinary family.'

'What about friends? I'd guess you have a pretty busy social life.'

'There's only Shelley, my mate from college. I don't go out much. I'm OK with my own company. I read, walk, that's about it.'

'No boyfriends?'

Why is he asking all these personal questions?

'Thanks for the coffee,' I say, and reach down for my backpack.

'Hey, sorry. I didn't mean to offend. Let's walk.'

He picks up the backpack, which begins to rock from side to side, making a chirping sound. Before I can stop him, he's opened the bag and is peering in. I try to take it from him, but it's too late. I hold my breath and feel my heart racing.

'Aha,' he laughs, reaching in and coming out with a fluffy toy owl. 'What have we here?'

I take it from him and put it back, zipping up the bag and slinging it over my shoulder.

'Just a kid's toy.'

As we follow the harbor wall, Josh puts a hand on my shoulder.

'Listen, Alice, I'm not trying to pry into your life. Don't get me wrong, please. I'm old enough to be your father, and I've noticed that over the last few weeks you don't seem to be as happy as you used to be. That worries me, and I hope you don't mind me saying so. If you need a friend to talk to, I'm here for you. I've got kids your age so I know a bit about life. Is there anything troubling you that I can help with?'

'No, thanks. I'm OK. There's nothing anybody can help with.'

We walk silently for five minutes, and then he says: 'You know, honey, people like Scorpio aren't like us. They live in a different world, and use us for entertainment. He's a nice enough guy, but there's no future for you there.'

I stop, and look at him with my mouth open.
'What!'

'Ah, well, we all saw you take him into the kitchen, and you were in there for a while, so, you know, we drew certain conclusions.'

I feel a flash of anger.

'Then you all drew the wrong conclusions. You don't really believe I expected a relationship with him, do you?'

Josh holds his hands up.

'Woah, I've got it all wrong. I'm glad to hear that. You seemed to be so high after that for a few weeks and then suddenly you lost your sparkle. I put two and two together and came up with five. My bad.'

I simmer down and give him a little smile.

'No worries. It's nice of you to care, Josh.'

'We all need somewhere to offload our problems. Would it offend you if I warned you about Sean?'

'Sean?'

'Well, I've noticed him hanging around you recently. Going on what I've seen before, he has a wandering eye and is always falling in love. The trouble is that he falls out of love just as fast. Thought I'd mention it. I wouldn't want to see you getting hurt.'

I laugh. 'Even if I was looking for somebody, he's not my type, so please don't worry!'

Josh shakes his head and gives a rueful grin. 'Wrong again! I'll keep my nose out of your life now Alice. It's only that I've seen such a change in you, I've been concerned.'

We walk for an hour. Josh tells me about his kids, how his wife died when they were small, and how he still misses her.

'Would you allow me the pleasure of buying you a lobster roll?' he asks, as we near a street vendor.

How can I resist? You know me and my perpetual hunger, but I don't eat anything that has a face. Luckily they do great tasting vegetarian alternatives these days. Sitting at a table overlooking the water, I start to relax. Josh makes me laugh. What he does with Decima is no concern of mine. I've kept so much bottled up for so long and if I'm honest I need somebody to talk to.

'Can I trust you, Josh? Not to share anything I tell you?'

'Alice, I swear to you that I will never repeat anything you tell me in confidence. I'm not that person. You can trust me.'

So I begin explaining how I'm worried about my parents because something strange is happening where they live, and then I find myself telling him how I'm in love with somebody who has married somebody else.

He nods as he listens, without interrupting.

When I finally stop, he takes my hands in his and looks at me with those kind blue eyes.

'You know, we humans often tend to worry about something that never happens. There may be nothing wrong out there, so try not to fret too much for now. Wait until you know there's something to worry about.'

He squeezes my hand. 'As for this man, he's a fool and he doesn't deserve you.'

Despite myself, I spring to Jai's defense.

'I'm the fool really. He never made any promises; I thought… Oh well, silly me. He comes from a different world.'

'What is he, an alien?' says Josh, trying to make me laugh.

I smile and shake my head. 'No, he's from India. He works here but he went back to his own country to get married.'

'Hm. Good looking Indian guy? I saw something in the Herald about that. Name like Jet?'

'Jai,' I say.

'That's the one. You know Alice, I'm a great believer that if something doesn't work out the way we want, later on when we look back, we realize it was for the best, because something better always comes along. I know how it feels when you lose somebody you love. It leaves a hole in you, and while it never completely heals, it does grow smaller in time. Hold on to your happy memories, but don't let them hold you back. There is somebody out there who is going to make you very happy one day. Don't close the door to them.'

I nod, but in my heart I know nobody will ever be able to replace Jai.

Josh glances at his watch.

'I'm due at my daughter's in an hour, so I'm going to love you and leave you, Alice. Thanks for your company and remember I'm always there if you need me.'

Walking home, I turn over Josh's words in my mind. Maybe he's right. Maybe I'm worrying about nothing and maybe one day I'll get over Jai. It was good to talk about it. As I turn to my apartment, I hear a whooshing noise and turn around to see somebody on a skateboard shooting past. It looks like Spike, I mean Sean. I am certain he is following me.

32

Wrong about Alice

Josh

It's time for some work on the house. These timber properties soon deteriorate without maintenance and this place is old now. Sometimes I'm tempted to sell up and move to somewhere smaller, more modern, but that would mean leaving behind all the memories of Diane, and the kids growing up here. And the views down to the ocean. I'd miss those. I guess I'll stay as long as I'm able to look after it. I go out to the shed and pick up a can of weatherproofing.

While I'm working, my mind goes back to Alice. I got it so wrong.

I was out for a jog along the harbor and saw her sitting there, looking so lost and alone. I almost kept going but something made me stop and walk over to her. She looked as if she was carrying the cares of the world on her shoulders. For a second I was going to walk away. Then she opened those big innocent blue eyes and drew me in, leaving me conflicted between feeling slightly paternal and rather horny. After Decima's exacting requirements, the idea of some simple loving with a pretty girl was interesting, but that sadness in her eyes – this girl needed help. But whoa! What would Decima do if she found out?

I went in heavy-handed, started grilling her too hard, and she closed down. Took a while to get her relaxed. What was she thinking hacking off all that gorgeous honey-blonde hair? And she's gotten so skinny. All her sweet curves have dropped away. I preferred her as she used to be.

There was something pretty odd going on. Her backpack was moving and making a noise. She seemed freaked out by it, so I opened it and there's a kid's toy owl. She looked so shocked, I guess it was something that has sentimental value for her, so I didn't comment.

We walked and talked and she slowly opened up. I can stop worrying about Sean, there's no interest on her side.

At least I found out what's troubling her. She's fallen for an Indian guy who seems to have encouraged her when he was already engaged to another woman. Mean bastard to play with such a naive girl. I explained to her that it was all for a good reason and something better was waiting for her in the future. I think that hit home. I hope so. She's a sweet kid.

Dang if I didn't spot Sean on his skateboard, following her home.

33

The bitch is in the building

Decima

The studio falls silent. All eyes are upon me.

I snap into smile. The light above Camera 1 turns from red to green.

'Welcome to The Witch's Hour.

But first. A word from our sponsors.'

An Estephe Gray purple passion lipstick fills the screen. I study it with a touch of nostalgia. This is probably the last time.

I look down at my freshly-manicured nails. Pointed falsies encrusted with jewels? No… Simple, trimmed down half moons covered with clear, bare varnish. Innocence itself.

Six, five, four…

The intro music fades. The green light appears. With a thundering heart, I take a deep breath.

Good afternoon, Hawk Bay City.

We have a different show today. No guests, but plenty to talk about. I hope you'll enjoy.

I adjust the collar of my white blouse, lining up tiny clusters of embroidered daisies each side. I cross my legs, as always, but my wool A-line maxi-skirt keeps itself tucked over my knees and my signature killer heels have been replaced with white Saint Laurent trainers.

I clear my throat and lean forward to the camera.

As you know, CGO TV and sponsors Estephe Gray have been bringing you the Witch's Hour 5 afternoons a week for several years now.

We love you, our loyal audience. We love our guests. I especially have had the privilege of entertaining them in my… Passion Pit… both during and after the show.

I twist my mouth into a grimace of disgust and hold it for a second. My natural acting ability is returning, full force with every 'sincere' word that I speak.

But now, it's time for a change.

My accent has taken on a life of its own. My voice comes out sounding somewhere between Kate, The Princess of Wales, and the landlady of an East End of London pub.

You see

PAUSE

It's time to come clean.

LONGER PAUSE

The truth is we've been operating under false circumstances.

Without any teleprompter, (I dismissed the operator earlier), I can see the shock and confusion on the cameraman's face.

There will be no more Witch's Hour.

There always comes a time for honesty. For the truth to be revealed… and I know, I know most sincerely, you will join me for this new adventure, this new phase of our journey.

No more pretense, ladies and gentlemen. No more hiding from the truth.

We all know, deep down, that witches do not exist any more than GHOSTS exist.

A stifled gasp from the cameraman as he twigs what I'm getting at.

But, further, we live in a time when hashtag MeToo is safely in the rearview mirror of ALL women's lives in this beautiful city, this wondrous part of the USA.

Women no longer have to fake their appearance, their appeal, for their NATURAL BEAUTY to shine through. It makes us no less women, it makes us MORE sensual, not less.

For is there nothing more beautiful than nature itself?

I have absolutely adored playing into the witchy game of magic, mystery and – above all – seduction with you, our loyal audience. Our guests have each loved us, as much as you do too. We have, for some time now, been able to get the most popular, the most sought-after celebrities in the region…. .

And I can assure you that that will continue. In the future. But… here's the thing. We're dropping the witchy fakery.

The fakery that I have been presenting myself to you through, will, from this day on, be as ditched as the make-up on my face has been wiped. In recompense, I will be more frank, more shocking, more MYSELF than you've ever seen me. Think LESS WITCH

MORE BITCH… that's me. That's the real me.

I actually spent an AGE this morning on the stuff that I have all over my face and eyes. It takes a tedious hour of hard work to 'look' natural. I flash a quick look down at my nails and up again.

I will ALWAYS be that bitch who asks the best questions, the awkward frank questions that you'd ask a guest if you were sitting here right with me.

I will continue to be your personal bitch on the screen. Truth, ladies and gentlemen, is even more important these days. I'm proud to say what we are all thinking so that you don't have to.

We cut to a commercial.

I watch the screen with nostalgia, wondering how long I have left. Estephe Gray would probably pull me right off air this minute if they could. But I can't stop what I'm saying. It feels so right. I will NOT let Lorelei Thornheart get away with it.

After the show, I grab Digby from his shelf and leave the building. By the time I get to the car my phone is trilling on repeat.

'That, Digby, is the actual sound of the crap hitting the fan.' I give Digby a pat on the head and tuck him safely out of earshot inside his Hermes bag.

'It's you and me, Digby. We're in control, old boy,' I click my seatbelt on and stare out of the window.

If the show goes to the wall, so be it. I'm my own person now. Maybe for the first time ever. I wiggle my toes. Whatever the end result, it'll be worth it to bring

Lorelei down.

And if the boys want natural, bare sexiness, Miss GoodyGoody Alice, well, I can play that game too. No more Scorpio. No more guest seductions. If we're still on air tomorrow, I'll simply up the bitch factor to make up for the lack of witch.

34

Pain and fear

Alice

I should have left it alone. Instead, when I got home, I googled 'Jai Mahan, Punjab, environmental research, marriage'.

There are two pages of links, but the first one, the one that hits me in the face, is on YouTube. Two and a half hours of the marriage preparations and ceremony.

At first I can't see Jai. I'm watching a celebration, with a great crowd of people wearing colorful clothes, bejeweled sarees, silk costumes. It is such a joyful scene, with music and dancing and tables of food. People are throwing rose petals at an exquisitely beautiful woman draped in a crimson saree embroidered with gold. She wears golden earrings, golden necklaces, golden bangles. She's crowned with a golden chain suspending a jeweled pendant on her forehead. Her hands and arms are painted in intricate designs. Her beauty is breathtaking. Her smile is radiant. There are English subtitles on the video. This woman is Jai's wife, Jasminder.

I know I should stop watching, but I must see Jai, I have to see him no matter how much it hurts.

A singing, clapping crowd appears surrounding a man with a neat black beard and mustache. He's dressed like a prince, in narrow cream trousers and a long cream embroidered silk coat studded with jewels. There's a cream turban on his head, a curved golden sword at his hip and a garland of crimson and yellow flowers around his neck. His beauty makes me catch my breath.

I'm thinking it must be the priest, or whatever they have there, but when the camera pans into his face I recognise Jai's eyes. He's walking towards the bride, with a proud smile and outstretched hands.

The full impact of our cultural differences hits me like a wrecking ball. The display of wealth and beauty blurs before my eyes and I feel tears rolling down my cheeks and bile rising into my throat.

We have nothing in common. We never did. I'm a plain working girl from a simple family, with hardly any friends, living in a dull apartment and working as little better than a slave. He clearly comes from a wealthy family, with a vast social circle and he's marrying an impossibly beautiful woman, the most beautiful woman I've ever seen.

I click YouTube off. I've seen enough, and the dream is over. He's never going to change his mind. I'm never going to see him standing outside my apartment. He is never going to turn and run and fly back to me. There was never a romance between us. It was nothing more than my foolish fantasy.

As Josh says, I have to let go and look ahead. I can't keep doing this.

I've forgotten Zylch, still zipped up in my backpack.

When I open it, he climbs out and trots to the kitchen.

'Hungry!' he calls.

*****

I decide to surprise my parents. Usually I let my mother know I'm coming so she bakes for me, but today I tuck Zylch into my backpack and **Broomstick** to half-way across the flats then walk the rest of the way.

I take a risk and let Zylch out. If he wants to be free, I won't stop him. However, he skips and hops along behind me, like a puppy.

There's a card parked outside the house, and when I reach the front door I hear raised voices, my father shouting and a door slamming, my mother talking rapidly.

The door swings open and an enormous, angry man strides out, shouting over his shoulder: 'You'd better think it over. And quickly. Don't test our patience and goodwill.'

Astrid runs behind him, and calls: 'And don't you ever come back here again.'

'Or what?' he laughs.

Then he trips over and falls on his back, waving his legs and arms in the air like a tortoise on its back as he rolls from side to side struggling to get back on his feet.

'Or you'll wish you hadn't,' she replies, walking into the house and closing the door.

He manages to turn onto his stomach and stand up, and then yelps and hastily pulls off his shoes. I know what my mother has done. She's cast the *Tumble* spell AND the *Shrink* spell, so not only has he fallen over, but his shoes have become two sizes too small.

Don't ever threaten Astrid!

Tottering towards his car, cursing as he stands on a sharp stone, he almost crashes into me. Zylch hisses.

'Who the **** are you?' he bellows.

I don't at all like his attitude, and I don't like that kind of language, so I invoke *Affliction*, which throws a stabbing pain into his ear.

He shakes his head and wipes a huge hand over his face, sobbing with pain.

I push past him and watch as he drags himself into his car. He grinds into gear and roars away, and just for good measure I send the *Deflate* spell after him to let his tyres down.

Don't ever, ever, threaten my family.

I find my mother is sitting at the kitchen table with her head in her hands. When she hears me she looks up and screams.

'Get out! Get out and leave us alone!'

'Astrid, it's me!'

'Alice! What have you done? You almost frightened me to death.'

Although we've spoken on the phone, she hasn't actually seen me since I cut off my hair and changed my look.

'You look like some kind of guerilla fighter. Terrible. What were you thinking?'

'I'm sorry. I didn't mean to scare you. Who was that dreadful man, and what is that about? I know something is going on, and I think it's time you told me.'

She sighs and stands up.

'I'll let your father explain. You're staying for lunch, I hope.'

She clatters around laying the table, uncharacteristically silent.

From the window I can see Zylch exploring the garden and playing with the plants.

'It sounded serious,' I say.

'Nothing for you to worry about. We will sort it out. Your father knows what to do.'

As Astrid dishes up the food, at precisely 1.00 pm, my father shambles into the room and slumps into his chair.

'Hello Dad,' I say. He looks up from his plate and notices that I'm sitting at the table.

'Ah Alice. Um. Where's your young man? I liked him.'

'He's in India at the moment,' I reply, keeping my voice light.

He takes a forkful of food, chews methodically, and nods in approval.

'I want to know what is going on here. Who was that man, and why was he shouting? I know something isn't right.'

Patrick continues eating until his plate is empty, then reaches for the cheeseboard. When he's cut himself a small slice, he leans back in his chair and looks at me.

'Nobody is going to force me out of my house.'

'Of course not. Why would they? Is somebody trying to do that? Is that why all the other houses have been sold?'

'They want to buy our house and knock it down. That is not going to happen. I am not interested in their money.'

'Who are they?'

'Our visitor did not give their name. He said, 'An interested party who will pay big bucks.'

'But why would they want our house? Is it the same people who've bought all the other houses here? Why? What do they want them for?'

'It seems there are some people who want to build a golf course and leisure center. A big project. It will cover the whole of the Brent Flats.'

'They can't do that! It's a protected zone, an area of ecological interest.'

'Big money talks. If you are rich enough and know the right people you can buy anything. But they are not buying my house. Over my dead body. That's it.'

He gets up and walks out of the room.

Astrid stares at me.

'I'm frightened, Alice. I'm really worried. I don't know how we're going to fight something as big as this.'

It's the first time I've ever known my mother to be afraid.

'Isn't there something you can do – you know, use your powers?'

'I don't have that kind of magic. Nothing that can deal with a situation like this. Whatever will we do if we're forced out? What will I do about the Screechers?'

I wonder if the organization Jai was working with concerning the protection of the ecology know about these plans.

'Try not to worry Mother. It will be OK. I have an idea.'

She shakes her head. I pat her on the shoulder, because that's what we usually do in our family, not being very demonstrative.

'Look,' I say, pointing out of the window where Zylch is lying on his back chewing a faded rose.

That raises a smile. 'Ha, that's a Zephrine. He has good taste; it's my favorite. Let me have a look at him.'

My mother probably keeps the untidiest house in the world, but her garden is spectacular and has twice had a double-page spread in *Beautiful Gardens* magazine. Through all seasons there is color and fragrance and when she isn't feeding the Screechers, or cooking, she's happiest outside humming, digging and pruning. My heart aches for her, imagining it being destroyed to make a leisure center.

I scoop Zylch up and bring him indoors. His silver coat is warm from the sunshine and smells faintly of earth. There's a pink petal sticking out of the corner of his mouth.

Astrid looks at him for a few seconds. 'Hm. He's turning into a very beautiful creature. I wonder how that's happened. What have you done with him?'

I explain how I thought I'd killed him, and how I had wept over his little body, and then found him alive. 'Could that possibly be the reason? Tears?'

'It's a thought. I'll do some research and see if I can find out anything more. I'm thinking that there could be a new market for Silver-coated Screechers. What do you feed him on?'

'He likes Parmesan cheese and peanut butter best, but he'll eat most things.'

'So no meat?'

'No, he eats whatever I eat.'

'Cheap to feed as well. This could be very interesting, Alice.'

She reaches out a cautious hand to touch him. Zylch purrs loudly. 'No aggression at all. It's an entirely different animal,' she muses, stroking his back.

Before I leave, I say, 'Please don't worry too much, Mother, about the house. I'm certain we can find a way to sort it out.'

'I'm not so sure,' she says. 'I have a very bad feeling. And Alice, for heaven's sake, stop wearing those ugly clothes, and get your hair sorted out. And I am very sorry about your Indian friend.'

I turn and stare at her. 'How did you know?' I ask.

'I'm your mother, of course I know. Why else would you make yourself look like that? I must admit I'm surprised, I sensed something there between you. It's a great shame. But please, Alice, dressing like that won't change anything.'

It's only as I'm going back into my apartment that I realize I forgot to tell her that Zylch really has started talking.

35

The plug is pulled

Decima

The show sponsors Estephe Gray Inc have indeed pulled the plug on us. As expected, Dad turned into a whirl of menace, throwing himself around the plane, Ornella said, doing his punching the walls trick.

Because of guest bookings, I've agreed to keep *The Witch's Hour* tag for the final few weeks we have left. It saves us getting sued all over the place by our advertisers. But nobody, though, *nobody* could stop me ditching the vampy seduction daywear for a neutral palette of bright white T-shirts, soft cream blouses, fresh cozy cottons, breezy natural blazers and leather flats along with my holier-than-thou English accent. Cool as anything. Screw the witch. Twice the Bitch Ice Cream Queen, that's me.

'What the actual!' was Josh's first reaction. He was the only one who saw it coming, one way or another, but he soon became pretty pleased with the way it's all turning out.

Me too. Lorelei Thornheart is only on her way to

ruin! She's disappeared! Insta, Twitter, YouTube, TikTok: all deleted. The 'church' has gone very, very quiet. She's got thousands of furious parishioners on her tail and so, so many questions are being asked in the media.

There's a new hashtag trending now, to #bringbacktheghost. It's like the whole world has turned on her, there's even a TikTok dance with a sheet. Ha ha, good luck with that, Lorelei.

Josh and the whole tech team's reputations are sky high and growing by the day as everybody's getting their theories in on how that 'witch' managed to fool everybody. We're all under strict instructions from Dad's legal team. No comments, no likes, no emojis allowed as the media frenzy takes hold.

I'm enjoying my new pure image and my growing notoriety. Our ratings are soaring and who knows where it could go? If they have any sense, Estephe Gray will have second thoughts when they see the viewing stats. But I'm keeping my eye on Zillow San Antonio house listings all the same.

As an added bonus, my sessions with the boys have become steamier and meaner than ever. I've started going all out on the slutty evening wear, just for them. The feeling that we're all on the rack is taking our bedroom games to new levels.

They're still taking it as a joke that I've declared that I'm going to be faithful to them and them alone, but this is truly the plan. Who needs the Scorpios of the world?

Sluts, the lot of them.

If all the plugs are pulled on all of CGO's shows and the Tower shuts down, I'm ready for it. I know a nice funky Hill Country house that's coming up for sale soon and the kind of work we will all be able to pull in should do us fine. We might even get a nice little Only Fans page going when we're settled.

Sean is a worry. He is getting more distant by the day. I don't know if he's noticed the changes to be honest. The other night I surprised him with my magic wand vibrator, and he kind of shrank in on himself, squeezed his legs together before slowly lifting one in the air and turning away. It was almost pompous. And no man, no man *ever* has shied away from my magic wand, built especially for the boys. Maybe my new sincerity is disturbing him? I tell you what, it's freaking Alice the freak right out. She's worried she'll lose her safe, cushy wushy little job and have to find work as a burger flipper or dry cleaner.

'That's life, honey,' I try to explain. 'And besides, we don't know what will happen yet. You need cheering up, girl.'

'I'm fine,' she says.

It's time to put my plan into action.

'No. I've been thinking. Listen… everybody's coming to mine on Saturday. Why don't you join us?'

She pulls a face. 'No thanks. Thanks all the same,' she backs away and scuttles off.

Josh is standing there shaking his head.

'She's moping, can't you see.'

'Course I can see. But honestly, she hasn't lost her job yet. And if she does, it's not the end of the world is it?'

'It's not that.'

'Well, what is it then?'

'What gets most young girls in the heart where it matters?'

Sweat prickles the back of my neck. 'Love?'

'She's got it real bad.'

'Sean?'

He shakes his head.

'None of you?'

He nods.

'Quit talking in riddles, Josh. What's going on?'

He looks over his shoulder. 'I'm not supposed to say.'

'Come on, spill the beans.'

'Boy she's been seeing. Thought he was about to propose to her, but turns out he's engaged to another back in India. Left her high and dry with barely a word.'

36

Ruin

Decima

Despite my optimism, the universe doesn't play ball. I'm despised now by everybody it seems: Dad. The boys. Ornella thinks it's hilarious that my show is on the way out. She's so thick she doesn't realize that Estephe Gray Beauty sponsors more shows than *The Witch's Hour* and our other advertisers are few and far between. Her days will be numbered too if the whole channel collapses.

Then, as everything gets worse by the day, Ornella announces her engagement. Torin! The pilot spy.

Her pilot as she now calls him. Dad's bemused but over the moon. He sees them all flying into the sunset for ever more on his beloved jet.

They're both rubbing it in my face, along with everything else.

Josh is being as strong and supportive as ever. He'll be getting amazing offers from the film industry coming in if he hasn't already. He *is* being a little coy about it when I ask. But that's business. Cory is such a cool Zen dude, he can get work anywhere any time. But Sean and Ramon are hopping mad. What have I done? What'll they do for work? I keep on telling them, we're going to make it *together*, it'll be *better* without Dad breathing down our necks. They both have ambitions and a move to San Antonio will make sense for them. I have it all worked out.

We'll share a cool house. We're a unit. They all need each other as much as they need me.

Actually, you know what? I'll come clean to you. All this bravado is hard work, even for me. Things are pretty scary right now. The whole station is going to the wall. Dad's got Ornella working the phones 24 hours a day cold calling every potential sponsor and advertiser on the West Coast. Nobody in the East wants to touch us. I'm relieved that the whole witch pretense is nearly behind me. San Antonio really could be the answer. I've got to keep the boys on side when I'm the reason they're all going to lose their jobs.

As for Alice, the permanent black cloud of gloom hovering over her is seeping out over everyone. She only has to shuffle into the room for the air to turn fetid and cloying. Nobody's letting on but I can sense everyone sighing at the same time. They're all being so stupidly *kind* to her.

What is she supposed to look like? The Girl With The Dragon Tattoo? The chopped hair and camo outfits? Hilarious!

I've made it clear that she will not be a part of my San Antonio plan. That's only fair. She'd be disappointed later if I were to say any different. Her family is here, after all, and she'll get a job downtown. I'm sure her beloved bagel store would love to have her behind the counter. Or there's that souvenir botanic gardens tea towel factory. They're always looking for people. Then she'll find a local guy at some point… Maybe.

'Life goes on, Alice. Get over it will you.' I wave my hand to shoo her out of the office one morning after the show, staggering on into its dying days.

Suddenly Sean is in my face. 'Enough of that now,' his arm is raised ready to grab me by the throat.

'Calm down, man,' I snap.

He freezes, and slowly lowers his arm but we're still eyeball to eyeball.

'Leave the girl alone now.'

'Come on,' I shrug. 'She's bringing us all down.'

'That's because we *are* all down. Thanks to you.' He snarls. He actually raises one side of his top lip and snarls at me.

Alice has her back to me, smirking her flushed little face off no doubt. I make to go for her, but hold on to my temper and stride off to the elevator instead.

The elevator isn't anywhere near our floor, so what's new? I take the stairs. There are some advantages to wearing trainers. When I reach Reception, Sean gets out of the elevator and grabs my elbow.

'We all got enough trouble as it is, Decima,' he says in the sing-song accent he knows I can never resist. He's cooled off already.

I turn to him, smile and cup his cheek.

'There's no need to rub it in, OK?' he continues. 'You know, Decima, it doesn't cost anything to be nice.'

How dare he. 'You really care for her, don't you?'

He shrugs me off.

'We all do,' he whispers. 'She's a friend.'

He frightened himself there, going for me like that. Sean's got a temper on him, we all know. But that was animal. Primal instinct. Protecting his loved one. This has got to stop. But how do you stop someone loving someone else?

37

Crisis of confidence

Decima

Since the whole of Hawk Bay City now knows I'm not a witch on a show we still have to call *The Witch's Hour*, faking it is impossible. I'm losing my touch, unsurprisingly with everything that's going on. Confidence begets confidence and all that. Today, one of the guests actually threw my questions back and started bitching at *me*.

I have taken to scuttling home and retreating into a long, hot bath. Whole bottles of my Insta spon Hollande Exotique's $70 Foam Fantastique are regularly going under the taps until the bubbles hit the ceiling. The way things are going, Hollande E will stop sending me freebies any day now so I might as well make the most of them.

I potter naked around the bathroom, checking my figure in the antique mirror propped up against the wall as I light a whole row of Estephe $100 candles. I sink into my souffle with a long, deep sigh. Not better than sex, but almost.

I am avoiding my phone as much as I can. The whole Lorelei controversy has cooled down as the news channels fix on Dad's other business interests. No more CGO TV seems certain, but is Dad's global business empire about to collapse too?

I click on Spotify which always gets Trevor dancing on the showerhead to 'his' song, The Divine Comedy's *National Express, Explicit Version*, bobbing his head manically to the chorus. I wish I could laugh. I wish I had somebody to talk to besides a crazy bobbing bird and an antique bear.

Friend. *Friend?* That was weeks ago but Sean's words are echoing, and I'm still wondering what to do about it.

When the steam has cleared, I reach out for my book and glasses, waiting faithfully for me on the chair beside the bath. A series by the *Zodiac Academy* Brit girls. A thick brick of a thing, and there are five more to come.

'Who needs friends when you've got books?' I say to Trevor. He hops down to the tap. It's touching. Like Digby, he would object to my disloyalty if he could, but he doesn't know the word 'friend'. Has no reason to hear it around here.

After struggling through a few pages, I throw the book across the room. I can't concentrate. I wish I had a friend. A dog would so do it for me. Since our little confrontation, even the phone sex with Sean has stopped. My choice. I don't want the humiliation of being rejected if I tried. The boys are pulling together more than ever now and even Josh is keeping his distance. It's costing me so much energy trying to keep hidden how vulnerable I'm feeling.

I'm hating that girl more and more. It's galling to see her getting all the empathy and kindness. Lapping it up, reveling in it. All the *friendship* crap. It's my own fault, I know. I work my body to the max because that's what I've got. And you have to work with what you've got haven't you? That's all anybody can do in this screwed up world.

The boys love our sessions, but they don't love me.

I *have* to stop this Alice infatuation nonsense if I'm going to keep it all together and get them to come with me to San Antonio. I'm scared. They're more inseparable than ever now all their jobs are on the line. Once the worries start there's no stopping them, is there? They're breeding in my brain like rats. Am I being paranoid now? I've no idea. And that's paranoia in a nutshell isn't it? The truth is that I've got to face up to the fact that if any one of them goes monogamous with Alice, if CGO TV falls, I really could be left on my own. Digby and Trevor are all very well but I will need *somebody* to love me In Texas, I could get a dog. I pick up my phone to check the latest realtor listings.

Oh no.

It's crazy what can happen if you leave your phone on its own for a few hours.

There's a disturbing email in from Lorelei

Thornheart. Or rather her lawyers. She's threatening me with legal action. Says she is a real witch. She'll prove it and make me pay for all her lost earnings and loss of reputation.

I forward the email to Josh and call him.

'You seen it?'

'I seen it, Decima,' he drawls.

'Well, don't sound so casual about it. What's going on?'

'I guess there's something I shoulda told you at the time.'

'WHAT?'

'The ghost.'

'What? You did fake it didn't you?'

'Yeah.'

I start to breathe again. Then stop.

'Yeah but…'

'But WHAT?'

'Lorelei, you see, she didn't want to do it.'

'She did though, didn't she?'

'Cliff made her. Made me too.'

'What do you mean?'

'Your dad tricked her, Decima. She never wanted to do it. Said it would ruin her reputation. That's why she left the show. She was so angry at Cliff. At how he'd tricked her.'

'But she's been clawing it in, built a whole religion around it! Until I stepped in with the truth that is.'

'The truth is, Decima. Lorelei *is* a real witch. As real as they come. She had no idea the ghost interview would be so popular. It made her so rich and famous she's run with the lie ever since. But she is a real witch, Decima. That's the truth of it. She can sue you to Kansas and back and will win.'

'She can't be!'

I snap my phone off, cutting him off in mid-sentence and turn on Digby. I pick him up and shake him by the shoulders so hard his button eyes spin. He looks deranged.

'You hear that, Digby? Now that really, really boils my blood.'

I throw him across the room. He just misses the fire. Trevor shrieks.

I race to him, gather him up and kiss him. 'I'm so sorry Digby bear, I'm so sorry…'

I fall to the floor, hugging him to me and sob long into the night.

I finally get to the bedroom, but I'm shutting down my phone when I see an Insta DM. An agent. Asking for a Zoom meet as soon as possible. The first message has been there a few days, some faker most likely, but a follow-up faker is unusual. I google her.

A proper website pops up. She's part of an agency in Spaulding Square, between Beverly Hills and Sunset Boulevard. There's a map, a contact email, a landline number. That all looks genuine. I scroll down. Offices in

London, Mumbai and Dubai.

I message her. She messages back. So far so real. She wants to meet but won't say anything more than that. The panic starts. What does she want? What if it's a scam? What if it's Lorelei? What do I wear? If she is real, is she interested in the vamp Decima or the new cool neutrals Decima? I need something right in between, and that means only one thing. Designer. Fresh designer. I call Magnolia Boutique Dress Hire. It's gone 11 but Sheenah picks up after two rings.

'Sheenah. Decima.'

'Hi babe, fancy hearing from you!' She pauses. Her voice goes soft, 'Sorry to hear about all the... the... well...'

I swallow hard. Sympathy is the *worst*. 'There's nothing to be sorry about.'

'You been getting some bad energy, babe.'

My chin wobbles. I push a finger behind my glasses to wipe a tear and open my mouth to pour my heart out but then close it again. 'I can't... talk about it, Sheenah.' That was close. Pull yourself together, Decima. You're talking to the gossip queen of Hawk Bay City here, she truly knows what everybody's thinking and who they're sleeping with before they do.

'What's the special occasion, babe?' she asks sweetly.

'I can't say.'

'Want to give us a little exclusive on what's going on over at CGO? A little 10% discount for an old friend?'

I stop feeling sorry for myself and get my bitch voice back. 'Sheenah, you're wicked but I haven't got time for this. I need a special outfit.'

'Is it for you my darling?'

'Who else would I be calling for?'

'Only asking my love. What sort of, er, occasion? I got some sensational Dior two pieces fresh in from Paris. Sewn by Galliano himself, so I've been reliably informed. Yours for a tidbit of info.'

'Nice try but you'll not get anything out of me. Dig out a Schiaparelli, will you, I'll drop by tomorrow.'

'Schiaparelli,' she hoots. 'Now that is a special occasion.'

As I'm slipping off to sleep, it comes to me. I remember my plan for Alice before all of this sponsor disaster kicked off: get her to mine and pull her into one of our special parties. Get her to join in. Once the boys know what they're not missing, the infatuations will stop. Parties have to have a reason, though. Well, that's easy. It'll be a leaving party for us all. We're all leaving for Texas. I'll announce my whole masterplan at the party. Alice will be upset that we're leaving her behind, but the boys and I will give her the time of her life to remember before we go. My parting gift to her.

The next morning, I message Sheenah before I go in.

You really are psychic aren't you. Double the booking time, I need to select outfits for two.

38

Karma?

Decima

Alice is suspicious. The silences between us get frostier the more friendly I become. I can help her, I tell her. If she wants to find Mr Right she needs to up her game. Sort out her make-up and clothes. I can see she's making an effort with her warrior look, but she really needs expert help. For a start, she uses a cheap mascara that leaves black marks around her eyes.

If she upped her budget and went for a different brand, it'd make so much difference.

'Here…' as I'm explaining, I take a tissue and go in to wipe a smudge.

'Please, no', she says, turning her head away.

I jump back with my arms in the air. 'I'm only trying to help you, Alice.'

'Thanks, but really, I'm good.'

I'm bad at this. Being friendly is not my thing. But I'm nothing if not persistent. The next day I try again. And the next. I keep going, wearing her down.

You know what? Maybe there is something to this karma stuff that Cory goes on about. I'm only a few days into my Alice charm offensive when that agent, "my new agent" as I'm telling everybody and anybody, comes through and I get the most incredible audition call ever. I can *not* believe it. I'm sworn to secrecy but now there's a *real* reason to party. I cannot sit still! I start the party preparations that night, baking brownies. *Baking Brownies.* That's the name of the bakery. I get a dozen on delivery. My boys all love 'my' brownies.

The next day I set them on a tray in the kitchen, dust them with my secret ingredient – a dash of Brit Tate & Lyle icing sugar – and seek Alice out. I find her sitting in her office. She looks so done-in. Her posture, her hunched shoulders, her wariness, her hands so sweaty they're damp. She's lost weight. I manage to compliment her on that and muffle some kind of an actual apology too as I shyly proffer the cake.

I'm not sure which did it, the chocolate, the apology or the compliment, but something gives in her. The smile in her eyes tells me she's softening towards me at last.

As she eats, I tell her about Saturday's party and some special treats I have thought of to cheer her up.

We hug it out. Something I've seen people do on reality TV shows, but have never experienced in real life beyond Digby. Digby's hugs are my go to hugs.

I work hard at keeping the bitch at bay and now even Sean's loving me, they're all loving me. Hugs all round.

Huggy wuggy hugs. Yuk. But I go along with it. For the time being.

39

Invitation

Alice

I turned down Decima's invitation to her house the first time, but now I'm seeing a different side to her. She was really sweet yesterday and came down to my 'office' with a tray of brownies. She perched on the edge of my desk and complimented me on my weight loss. Under that horrid public persona, I can see the kind person I always suspected was there. I think that now the pressure to pretend to be a witch is no longer there, she's much happier. I am happy for her, and so pleased that she's making such an effort to make up for her bitchiness.

Apparently, she has some amazing news to share, and she wants all the team – that's the boys and me – to be there to hear the news so we can celebrate together. She's paying for me to have a full beauty treatment and a new outfit as a thank you for the way I have worked for her.

She said: 'Alice, I'm afraid I haven't been very nice to you, and I want to apologize. I'd like to make it up to you if you'll let me.'

My heart melted. I'm not the kind of person who holds a grudge. I like to get on with everybody. I said: 'Decima, there is no need to apologize. I enjoy working for you and I know yours is a very high-pressure job and you've had a rough time. It's lovely to see the real you.'

She stood up and held out her arms and we had a long hug.

'I've asked Cory to bring you on Saturday, so you won't need a cab. He'll pick you up at 7.30. Don't eat – I've taken care of everything. I know how you love your food! All you have to do is turn up looking lovely.'

I thought the comment about me loving my food was a little pointed, but to be honest this invitation couldn't have come at a better moment. I can't seem to pull myself together and get over Jai. As much as I try, I still feel hollow inside, all the time. Maybe this is what I need, an evening among friends.

For the second time in my life, I've been pampered and dressed in amazing clothes. I try not to think about the last time.

Decima arranged for her own beautician to give me a head-to-toe treatment. I'm steamed, oiled, massaged, polished and painted and it felt rather wonderful to let myself go completely and enjoy the moment. Her hairdresser sorted out my chopped locks into a classy Pixie cut. I'm still getting used to not having my hair touching my shoulders. I do like the new style, although I need quite a lot of eye make-up to balance it. I am so grateful to Decima.

I have to check twice the address of the boutique she is sending me to, as it's out of town and in a private house. There's no signage outside, so I ring the bell cautiously.

An elderly woman with straggly hair opens the door and stares at me.

'Uh, sorry, I think I have the wrong address.'

'Have you been sent by Decima?'

'Yes. I thought it was a boutique.'

'Come in,' she says, waving me through the door. 'Wait here.'

I stand in the hall. A door opens at the end of the passage, and a smiling young woman beckons me.

'Hi babe! You must be Alice. I'm Sheena. Come on down here.'

She leads into what looks like an ordinary living room, with a long mirror against one wall.

'So, it's for a special party, yes? Well, I have the very thing for you,' she says. 'Not many people can wear something like this, but it's totally made for you. Decima filled me in and I think you'll see she has picked out the perfect look for the night.'

She opens a cupboard door and pulls out something red and glimmery.

'Um, is this actually Magnolia Boutique? I was expecting it to be a shop?'

Sheena gives a tinkly laugh. 'Yeah, I know. It's kinda

weird, no? We are not your normal fashion outlet. Our clients wouldn't be seen dead going into commercial premises with fancy lighting and silver furnishings. We only cater for the highest-end customers and celebs who demand absolute privacy and discretion. Check out the glossy mags – when you see somebody wearing something stunning, and there's no designer tag, then you know it comes from Magnolia.'

'Oh wow! That's pretty exclusive!'

'Right on babe. Now, I'm going to leave you some privacy so you can try this on and see what you think. Ring the little bell when you're ready,' she points to a small silver bell on a coffee table, and I'll be back. You want a coffee?'

'Thanks. White and two sugars. Oh no, one sugar please.'

Sheena hooks the red glimmery thing over a peg on the back of the door and brings me a mug of coffee; then with a little wave she closes the door behind her.

There's a price tag attached to the dress. $6,000. There's hardly any fabric. It's like a scarlet spider's web. Shredded fabric encrusted with diamonds, held around my neck by a scarlet ribbon. There is no back, no sleeves, and it ends at mid-thigh. The bust area is lined with a narrow strip of scarlet chiffon. There's a tiny scarlet thong that goes with it. (I hate thongs, so uncomfortable, but as Sheena points out, if I don't wear something down there everybody will see my lady garden and I can't wear my normal boy shorts.)

Getting this dress on is quite a struggle, because my hands keep going between the webs, but eventually it falls into place.

It's a perfect fit, but I'm virtually naked and look like a slender stranger about to step onto the catwalk, or possibly the center page of a girlie magazine. There is no way I could ever wear this in public. I ring the little bell.

Sheena gasps when she sees me.

'Wow! Decima was so right. You look like a million dollars, no, ten million dollars.

'Are you sure this is OK for me?' I ask. 'It feels like I'm naked.'

'Absolutely honey. You look ravishing. Just as Decima asked. Trust me. With your looks and body, you can wear anything. You are going to feel like a star in this. You'll stop the traffic. All you need is a little confidence in yourself. Think how many women would kill for a look like this. Decima wanted you to have the very best. She's a great fan of yours.'

Maybe she's right. It is an incredible outfit and I do feel powerful. I need to get out of my shell and start living.

'Well, thanks Sheena, you've put my mind at rest.

'Ever thought of having a vajazzle?' she asks.

'A what?'

'Down there. Wax it and jazz it up with crystals. My sister is a vajazzle artist. She could do a beaut for you. Take this.' She hands me a card with a photo of a female private area completely covered with glittering flowers and butterflies.

There's a lot I don't know. I remember how I had it waxed once and it was agonizingly painful.

She produces a pair of diamante sandals I can barely walk in.

'They're so high! I'll fall off them.'

'No, you won't, babe. You'll get used to them very quickly. They're party-wear, you won't be walking around much.'

Sheena gives me a big hug.

'Have a great time. Knock'em dead!'

40

The party

Alice

I'm ready and waiting when Cory arrives to collect me for Decima's party. I've flip-flopped between thinking I look amazing, and thinking I look ridiculous in this outfit. One minute I feel confident, and the next terrified. Thinking of how much Decima has spent on me, I owe it to her to go out there and carry it off.

Luckily it's a cold, damp evening, which gives me an excuse to throw the blue velvet cloak Shelley made for me last Christmas over the spider dress.

As usual Cory is very quiet. He's never been much of a talker, and I've never really got to know him. He's quite an aloof and private person, with an amazing aristocratic accent, like Jeremy Irons, the actor. He'd fit in fine in one of those British palaces or castles, mixing with royalty, so I don't know what brings him to this place.

I ask if he knows anything about the announcement tonight. He shakes his head.

'We'll know soon enough. I only know that Decima

has good news for us.'

'I do hope so. I've been really worried.'

He doesn't reply, so we sit in silence until we reach the gates into the complex where Decima lives. Two uniformed attendants ask for Cory's permit, and while one checks the car the other talks into his phone.

'Is there something wrong?' I ask.

'It's normal. Nobody gets in here until they've passed security. Look up there – see all those cameras? You can't get in or out of these gates without being seen. The perimeter wall is 10 ft. high and topped with electric wire. With all the crime around town, the residents here don't take any risks.'

The guard hands him back his permit and waves us through the gates.

The landscape here is scary. It's so perfect. The manicured lawns, the uniform palms, not a leaf out of place. Looks like every piece of gravel has been hand polished and you'd be shot if you walked on the grass.

Decima's house is the furthest in the complex, with its own security – an electronic gate mounted with CCTV cameras, and a stone wall reinforced with razor wire.

Cory grimaces and says: 'One of the problems of being a celebrity – protecting your privacy. A mouse can't get in or out of here without being seen.'

The cameras swivel around and click as the gates slide open. Cory drives through, parking his little car alongside Decima's Porsche. He opens the door, hands me out onto the polished gravel and leads me up the steps to a front door which opens out into a wide hallway with a checkered marble floor.

A tall man in a tuxedo steps forward.

'Welcome,' he smiles. 'May I take your cape, Madame?'

I grasp it tightly. 'No, thank you. I'll keep it until I'm a little warmer.'

'There's a fire in the living area,' he says. 'You'll soon be warm. If you would like to go up,' he points to a curved wooden staircase.

Cory takes my elbow and leads me up and into a cozy wood-paneled room lined with bookshelves. There are thick wool rugs scattered on the floor, and soft furnishings in rich jeweled colors. Table lamps cast soft warm light onto piles of books. Above the fireplace is a portrait of a woman. At first glance I think it's Decima, but I go for a closer look and see that, although this woman has Decima's eyes, she has a little turned up nose, unlike Decima's beak, and faint lines around her eyes.

'Alice! Darling! You're here! How wonderful. Thank you so much for coming tonight.'

Decima puts an arm around my shoulders.

'My mother,' she says, pointing up at the painting.

'I can see the likeness,' I reply. 'You're very like her.'

'Apart from the nose that I inherited from my father,' she chuckles.

I say: 'You have always reminded me of somebody

and I'm sure I recognise your mother. I've seen pictures of her somewhere.'

'My mother was Graciela Mazellini.'

'The ballerina?'

'The *prima* ballerina.'

'Oh yes, now I remember. And your father was a racing driver, wasn't he?'

'Yeah.' She turns away and gives Cory a peck on the cheek. 'Welcome, my English prince,' she murmurs. 'I hope you will enjoy this special evening.'

I stand there staring at the portrait, searching my memory. There was something ten years ago, it was big news at the time. A scandal? I'll have to look it up.

Ramon, Sean and Josh arrive together. They walk over to Decima and kiss her. Sean comes and stands beside me. When I smile at him he flushes.

'Ah, we're all here. How lovely. Grant, would you like to serve the drinks now?' Decima looks over at him, he nods.

So this is her new fake butler Sean told me about… some kind of handyman from the complex that she's hiring by the hour to make her look fancy and massage her ego even more. I hesitate when he offers me a drink from a tray. I'm not used to drinking alcohol. Decima smiles. 'It's safe, Alice, mainly fruit juice. Just a little refreshment.'

I sip the glass and relax. It's delicious. Pineapple and mint, with a touch of something sour to counteract the sweetness.

Away from the studio, Decima seems relaxed and happy, a totally different person. She sits on a sofa with her legs curled up, smiling as Grant hands around trays of finger food. I would never have imagined her in a house like this, so different to her work environment where she is usually hard and unpleasant.

I've hung on to my cloak, keeping it wrapped around me. I say to Decima 'I hope you don't mind, but I'm feeling cold.'

'You keep wrapped up Alice,' she says. 'Whatever makes you comfortable. Come and sit close to the fire. Grant, put some more logs on please.'

Sean keeps staring at me. He seems anxious, his fingers fiddling and pinching at his jeans. I give him a little smile, which seems to make him even more nervous, so I go over and sit next to him.

'Hey, Sean, are you enjoying yourself? Isn't it exciting! I wonder what news Decima has for us?'

He's silent for at least a minute, then he turns to me and says quietly: 'Alice, I have a very bad feeling.'

'What do you mean?'

'I can feel it. There's something wrong.'

I put my hand on his knee and give a squeeze. 'Don't be silly. What could be bad? It's a celebration!'

'Alice, if I call a cab, will you let me take you home? Believe me, my gut feelings are never wrong. Something very, very bad is going to happen tonight.'

There's desperation in his voice, and I'm about to ask him what he is expecting, when Decima comes over.

'Come on guys, time to hear the good news.'

She pulls Sean up away from me before he can say any more.

I'm beginning to feel uncomfortably hot after half an hour sitting near the fire and accept another drink from Grant.

Decima claps her hands quietly, and the room falls silent.

'You all know what CGO TV stands for don't you? Cliff Gauld Ornella, named after his beloved daughter and companion, my sister Ornella. Well, guys, prepare for a station rename to CGD TV, because… I am now the favored one.'

I think she means the saintly one. She's got her hands steepled in front of her like she's praying and she's looking slowly around at us all like a priest giving a sermon. I catch Sean's eye. He's frowning.

'I'm teasing,' she continues. 'That's never going to happen. But I'm really thrilled to announce that we are saved. We have a new sponsor, guys, we've come through the crisis and we're out the other side smelling of… well, I'll get to that. We're going GLOBAL.'

She pauses again. We're all looking at each other and back at her. I've never seen her more radiant.

'Don't all look so happy about it!'

'We're in shock,' says Josh.

'For real?' says Sean. 'We're really saved?'

Cory doesn't say anything, but he's looking as confused as the rest of us.

'We're more than saved. Terikhan Dubai Beauty will be sponsoring me, and my new show, *The Bitch's Hour*, with unlimited dollars. Enough to run the whole station without the need of Estephe's cents.'

Josh is already googling. He looks up from his phone. 'Guys, guys, guys, she's not kidding. They're mahoosive.'

Decima nods. 'They are seriously loaded. They make a perfume called TO ME with a strap line of SAY IT LIKE IT IS. A nod to all the #MeToo women of the world. Mature, honest and gutsy. Above all, *honest*. No deceptions. No lies. The truth hurts, bitch. That's the line. It's been a big hit in Europe and Asia and they've been searching the US for the American Face to launch.'

With that nose? We're all thinking it.

She must have read our minds, as she goes on. 'A woman who is so much more than beauty. Bringing together the holy trinity of beauty, ugliness and terror. A woman who encapsulates the strong women of the world. Who is not afraid to stand up for herself. A woman who says it like it is: the truth. No matter the consequences. Who is not afraid of asking difficult questions of her guests.

Our guests will be strong, gutsy women from all over the world. Not just three-bit singers, YouTubers, cooks and writers, but businesswomen, politicians, world leaders, entrepreneurs, wellness gurus. We'll be part of the global digital discussion, reaching millions of viewers.'

'Up the Bitch and CANCEL THE WITCH,' she throws both arms in the air.

We all clap and cheer, and she takes a little bow and announces that she has arranged a special surprise to celebrate the great news.

She smiles at me, and says: 'I couldn't do my job without the help of my wonderful right-hand woman, Alice. Come over here,' she beckons me with her finger.

Blushing with embarrassment I go and stand beside her. I'm feeling a little woozy

'Can we all show our appreciation for this lady who works so hard behind the scenes. And she has a special treat for you tonight, gentlemen.'

She wraps her arm around my shoulders and without warning tugs my cloak so it falls to the floor, leaving me standing there in the red spider web.

Ramon is the first to react, with a gasp and a long whistle.

Cory and Josh look horrified.

Sean rushes up to me and tries to pick up the cloak. As Decima is standing on it, he can't, so instead he wraps his arms around me. I think he's attacking me and push him away violently so that he falls onto the floor.

Decima is clapping her hands and laughing.

I reach down for the cape, but she's keeping her foot on it.

'Please, Decima,' I say, tugging at the cape.

Sean has stood up and is standing with his back to me with his arms outstretched to the side, trying to shield me from the others.

'Let's party, everyone,' screams Decima, grabbing me by the hand and dragging me up close to the men. 'Whose first to give Alice the loving she's looking for?'

She's gripping me so hard. The more I struggle the harder she holds me, digging her nails into my wrist.

'Decima! For pity's sake. What are you doing?' shouts Josh.

Cory joins Sean and tries to shield me as Ramon takes a step forward. Josh pushes him away hard so he loses his balance and bangs into a table.

Decima's eyes are glinting dangerously. 'How dare you humiliate Alice when she has made such an effort.'

'No, please. I don't want this,' I stutter, trying to wrench the cloak back off the floor.

'Alice, I've seen the way the boys and you look at each other. You know this is what you've always wanted. Tonight I'm making it a reality for you. I'm not possessive, you can take whichever of them you want. Come on guys, don't be shy! Cory – you go first; I can see you can't wait.'

'Is that so, Decima? Then I tell you what – find somebody else. I will not be part of this disgusting charade.' Cory's cut glass voice slices through the noise.

'NO! Leave her alone! Let her go!' Sean roars,

charging at Grant and trying to push him away from the door. But Grant is too strong and easily holds Sean at arm's length, laughing.

'Now come on everyone, where's your sense of fun? This is a party, right? So party!' Decima jerks me around and then pushes me hard so I fall to the floor and have to struggle back to my feet, my hands entangled in the dress.

Sean wrestles madly, with tears rolling down his face, as Grant holds him back.

'This is not funny Decima,' Josh snaps. 'It's not funny at all. Let go of the poor girl.'

'Oh dear, what a load of party poopers you are. It seems I'm going to be needing a whole new team, and you're all going to be looking for somebody else to hire your sorry arses.'

I'm frightened. Everybody here is afraid of her, of what she will do next. The guys are going to lose their jobs. I have to do something very dangerous. If I fail, I will probably die.

Envisioning to move from one place to another is straightforward and something I do fairly often, but only when there is nobody around to see. The presence of muggles depletes magical energy to a dangerous level. I may not have enough for what I'm about to try, and I'm feeling the effect of alcohol dulling my focus.

I stand very tall, very still, looking straight ahead at the wall lined with bookshelves. I take deep breaths and count aloud to ten while silently summoning *Sesame*

Fortissimo – a spell I have never used before, to allow me through the toughest obstacles. Nobody moves. The men are staring at me, holding their breath. Decima giggles.

I close my eyes and imagine myself through the wall.

For a moment nothing happens, and then the room shimmers. I feel momentary resistance from the books, the timber, then the bricks scraping at me. Will they let me through? Briefly I panic, until I feel a blast of cold air as I land on my back in the garden below.

From above Decima is screaming, shouting, 'Where the HECK has she gone! Find her!'

A door slams and I hear footsteps running down the staircase. The front door flies open and the men scatter through the garden, running straight past me.

I press myself against the wall, into the shadows, panting silently, trying to summon more power. I hear them pushing aside the bushes, grunting, calling my name, but I stay close to the wall, holding my breath and shivering from the cold.

A pair of feet stop in front of me and I look up into Sean's startled eyes. Wordlessly he takes off his jacket and drapes it tenderly around my shoulders. I mouth a silent 'Thank you,' before he runs to catch up with the others.

Without my phone I try using the old-fashioned **Broomstick** spell, but I don't have enough energy left to make it work. I'm trapped in the damp flower bed wondering how, and how long it will be before I can escape.

A high-pitched howl makes me jump, as the garden is lit with searchlights. 'Intruder alert. Intruder alert,' blares an alarm. I hear the gates grinding open and running feet crunching across the gravel.

Decima is screaming: 'Somebody's out there! Shoot to kill!'

Crouching in the shadows, shaking with fright, trying in vain to summon something, anything to protect myself, I have a bizarre thought. If I'm shot dead, and my picture is all over the news, what will my parents think when they see my body in the spider dress? Will Jai see it?

Very slowly I slip into Sean's jacket. At least most of me will be covered. The running feet are getting closer, men shouting to each other. I know they have guns. As the full glare of a searchlight fixes on me I feel a strange calm, knowing this is how it ends. No more fear. I hope it will be quick. How I wish I could have kissed Jai once before I died.

41

Now it's your turn

Decima

'Good night, was it?' Sheena takes the tote bag of costumes and shoes from me and spreads my gown over the counter.

'Of course it was, it was my party wasn't it?'

Her eyes narrow. She glances up.

'Something to celebrate, then,' she says as a statement, almost to herself.

I immediately regret what I've said. Information. Manna to this woman.

'Heard there was some kind of disturbance out at Eagle's Nest way last night.'

I fish for my phone and scroll without answering.

'You don't expect that in a "gated community" do you?' She pushes. 'Isn't that what they're for?'

I keep scrolling.

'To keep the riff raff out?'

'That's why it was probably a false alarm, Sheena.'

Humming lightly, she busies herself with her giant magnifying glass, checking my gown for damage that she

231

can charge me a fortune for.

I'm tempted to distract her with my positive news but I don't want to jinx it. I was a little ahead of myself with my announcements. Nothing has been signed with Dubai yet. But my new agent Gwendoline has got our own contract between us sorted and was very keen to get it signed. She wouldn't do that unless she knew it was greenlit. So I am believing it. I am going to have *carte blanche* to up the sophistication, screw the bitch in me, and nobody, not even Dad, will be able to stop me.

Sheena puts my gown in her laundry basket, picks up the spider costume with the tips of her fingers, snaps a pedal bin open with her foot and drops it in from a great height. The bin closes with a clang.

'Halloween tat, what will they come up with next?' she throws her eyes to the ceiling. 'I don't like having it in, contaminating my style, but sometimes you got to go with what the customer demands. You've just proved it, haven't you? She giggles.

'Good riddance to it.'

'Was she taken in by the $6,000 label?'

'Oh yes. She's not very bright.'

Sheena cackles.

I'm glad to see the back of it. What a devious little creature that girl is. Well, guess what Alice, it doesn't matter any more. You've shown the boys what you're made of, you silly, weak creature. I think we've seen the last of you, and I've got them in my pocket now. And that includes Sean.

To be safe, I did have to grovel a bit. I know. So painful. Nothing more than a bit of fun, I said. A harmless joke. I know how much I get from our sessions, I truly thought she'd be up for the experience. A once-in-a-lifetime opportunity. As for Alice. How, I hinted, do they think she got into that costume without being in on it? So no squirming, and no danger, Sean's temper flares being what they are lately.

And the disappearing act? Getting past two sets of security? I admit I don't know how she did that and it was pretty spectacular. I'm guessing she had a little help from somebody, but who? I'll find out eventually. My money's on Josh, given he's the magic ghost special FX wizard around here. Perhaps I shouldn't trust him too far? Ramon mentioned that he'd seen Josh and Alice together down at the harbor. Something going on behind my back? Hm. And Josh mentioned that he'd found out something about her pathetic 'love life' so he must have been spending time with her. I'm going to start keeping an eye on him.

Little Miss Disappearing Act, it's within my power to fire you now and get you out of the boys' way altogether, but I actually would rather have some fun before I do. You've made my life difficult these past months, now it's your turn. But that's only if you are dumb enough to turn up for work on Monday after making such a fool of yourself. Which I very much doubt. Good riddance!

We're all going to be very, very rich indeed. Except you. You are going to be nothing.

42

Change

Alice

I feel a creeping warmth and see a blurred whiteness above me. It feels very peaceful. Am I dying? Dead?

There is something inside the whiteness, something slightly familiar. I screw up my eyes to focus on it, and realize it's the light fitting on the ceiling of my bedroom. I wiggle my toes, then my fingers. I'm definitely not dead and I don't feel any pain.

A large shadow moves past the end of the bed.

'Shelley?' I call. 'Mother? Is somebody there?'

There's no reply.

I push away a cover and swing my legs over the edge of the bed and look around. There's nobody here, except Zylch, sitting on a chair in the corner of the room, watching me with amber eyes.

My head feels fuzzy and there's a sour taste in my mouth. I take a bottle of water from the fridge and sip it while I try to clear my thoughts.

Catching sight of myself in the bedroom mirror, I see

I'm wearing Sean's jacket over the red spider dress, and it all comes back to me.

The party at Decima's house. The heat of the fire, the sweet drinks, Sean's premonition. Decima's crazed behavior, the horrified reaction of the guys, and my escape from the room.

I remember shivering in the garden as men with guns searched for me, my feeling of helplessness as I waited to be shot.

And then I remember something else. I remember being lifted in strong arms from the flowerbed, folded against a warm silken body with a familiar smell, and being lifted into the night, over the walls, away from the shouting and the lights, and feeling safe.

I pick Zylch up, turning him on his back and examining his paws. Between the toes of his back feet I find specks of damp garden soil.

He stares up at me, and from the depths of his eyes I see so much love reflected. I hold him tightly as my tears splash over his body, rocking him until I fall asleep.

It's still dark when I wake. I lay Zylch down, and then I peel off the spider's web dress and carefully fold it back into its bag, with the shoes. I shower, pick up my phone and **Broomstick** back to Decima's house. All the lights are out and I can hear a regular snoring. I collect my cloak and leave the dress and shoes on one of the sofas. Let her work that out.

Back home again, I'm too hyped to sleep. I sit by the

window listening to the distant drone of traffic.

What was Decima thinking? Is she mad? Drugged?

I turn it over and over in my mind, thinking how I should have dealt with the evening differently. What could I have done, what should I have done?

It comes down to the spider dress. If I had any guts, I'd have refused to wear it. It was disgusting, I knew that, and I meekly allowed Sheena to persuade me.

Yes, that's what I am. Meek. Weak. Always letting people push me around. First Rory, then Decima, then Sheena. Just cruising through life, always taking the line of least resistance, the easy route.

Enough is enough. I'm almost 26 years old. I have to stop being a victim and stand up for myself. But can I? After all these years, can I really change my mousy nature?

I'm staring at my reflection in the window when Zylch's face appears over my shoulder.

'Yes, you can. Courage, Alice,' he says.

I realize I've been talking aloud.

I stroke his floppy ears and rest my face against his.

'Really, Zylch? Can I?'

'It's in your hands. If you fall, I will pick you up. Now is your time.'

Is it my imagination, or do I feel a pulsing in my veins, as if my body has somehow tightened, become stronger? The reflection in the window looks back at me with a new calmness and assurance.

When I arrive at work on Monday, it's with my head

high and my shoulders back.

The stallions look at first shocked, and then embarrassed. I give a big smile and say: 'Hi guys, how was your weekend? Ready for a good week? Let's smash it. Another day, another dollar!'

I pour myself a coffee and walk into my cubicle for the last time. I'm not going to be shut away down here, I'm moving up to the top with Decima. She simply doesn't know it yet.

I hear the elevator ping, and her heels smacking into the floor. She walks into the cubicle with an armful of roses and a wicker hamper.

'Alice, how on earth do I apologize for Saturday? I believe somebody must have spiked my drink to make me behave like that, but there's simply no excuse. I can't expect you to forgive me.'

There are tears in her eyes. Crocodile tears.

'Honestly, I feel like cutting my throat. I am so, so ashamed.'

She's managed to make the tears trickle down her cheeks. That's the actress in her.

She hands me the flowers and heaves the hamper on my desk.

'There's no way I could ever adequately apologize to you. I totally understand you'll want to leave, although we'll all miss you terribly.'

I see what you're doing, Decima.

The stallions have come out from their room and are

standing behind her in the doorway. I give them a little wave. Decima glances back over her shoulder, looking irritated. She hisses something under her breath.

'Of course, I'll give you the best, most glowing reference. Anybody will be blessed to have such a wonderful PA. If only I could turn back the clock, find some way to make it up to you, but I trust this' – she indicates the hamper – 'will show you how much I've valued you. It's a luxury cheese range. I hope you'll enjoy it.' She shrugs ruefully. 'There's a lovely porcelain cheese plate and knife, too, to remind you of all of us here at The Tower. Come and give me a hug before you go.'

I stand up. 'It's OK, Decima. It's fine. There's no need to apologize, and I'm certainly not leaving. I love my job here too much.'

I look her straight in the eyes and meet her glare with a smile.

She sees. She sees I'm not defeated, she knows she can't fire me. She cannot break my contract. Only I can decide to leave, and I'm not going anywhere except up.

She pinches her lips together and raises her eyebrows. 'Well, I must say I'm surprised. I'd have thought after we've all seen you um, virtually naked, you'd be too uncomfortable to want to stay.'

'I think there are more important things to deal with now, getting the new show up and running. We are all going to need to focus on that. I'm going to pretend that Saturday night was just a dream. I shall wipe it out of my mind and concentrate on working with you on *The Bitch's Hour*. You can rely on my total support and 100% commitment. I'll need to move back to my office on the 17th floor, so I'm nearer you and more involved with the programme, like it says in my contract.'

I stare hard at her and for the first time I notice a flicker of uncertainty in her eyes.

'Of course. If you're sure that's what you want. I'll have your office organized for you,' she says with a brittle smile. 'It will be ready tomorrow.'

'Thank you so much Decima, and for the lovely flowers and hamper. I'll sort out my stuff down here and join you upstairs tomorrow. I can't wait to be more involved.'

She turns on her heel, her fists clenched to her sides, pushing her way past the boys, and clacking back towards the elevator.

Change is coming at The Tower. For a start, a real witch will be part of the programme. I feel my face break into a huge smile.

43

Touché, Decima

Josh

I keep thinking things can't get any wilder, and then that happens.

We're hanging in the basement, planning the week ahead. We've all been thinking of Alice, poor kid, when she puts her head round the door bright-eyed and bushy-tailed and says: 'Hi guys! Another day, another dollar!' As if Saturday night never happened! And, while I think of it, what went on there? That was totally humdingingly crazy. She seemed to disappear straight through the freaking wall.

She skips off back to her little office, leaving us open-mouthed, staring at each other in astonishment. In truth I don't think any of us imagined she'd be back, let alone buzzing. Sean is making a funny humming noise in his throat.

The CCTV picks up Decima coming out the elevator pushing a trolley and looking smug. She stops outside Alice's cubicle and unloads a bunch of flowers and a hamper. What the…!

We creep out and gather silently around the doorway behind her. Alice gives us a little wave, and Decima turns and sees us standing there. She scowls and hisses 'Get lost,' but we're not going anywhere.

She's putting on a great act, shaky voice, fake tears, fake apology to Alice, who's actually looking slightly amused.

Sean starts to whimper.

'When Alice goes, I'm out of here,' he sobs. 'I'm out of here.'

I'm thinking that I've had enough of Decima, too. Time to move on. This place has become too toxic.

And then Alice stuns us all. She outplays Decima.

44

Shell shocked

Ramon

I'm still processing the craziness of the last three days.

What was Saturday night about? Alice dressed like a cheap hooker. Was she in cahoots with Decima? Playing hard to get? Was it some kind of test? Decima offering her to us on a plate, I can't get my head around that. Alice must have known what she was doing. Did she get cold feet? Is she a tease?

Sean was out of his mind, Decima was laughing hysterically, Cory and Josh stood there like a couple of dummies not knowing what to do. I didn't know if I was meant to make it with Alice, if that's what Decima really wanted, but at the same time it felt as if she didn't want it. Anyway, Alice looked terrified and there was no way I'd have been able to. Never have forced any woman and never would. It was too bizarre.

And then pouff! Alice vanished. Literally disappeared, without even a puff of smoke. Was that all some fancy trick arranged by Decima and Josh? Josh swore he knew nothing about it, and I had to believe him. He seemed genuinely as shocked as I was.

I called Sean but he didn't want to talk. It sounded as if he was crying.

He was at Mass on Sunday. On his knees the whole time. When it was over I tapped him on the shoulder and asked if he was coming for a drink, but he shook his head and whispered he was talking to Jesus.

Then Decima got us all on WhatApp and apologized if we'd misunderstood her joke. She explained it was only meant as a bit of fun, for all of us to let our hair down knowing that our jobs were safe. She hadn't realized Alice would take it so seriously, and she's really truly sorry and demands our forgiveness if she was out of line. Of course, we all accepted her explanations, even if privately we had our doubts.

Monday morning we are all in early, talking about Saturday night and agreeing that there was no way Alice would be back after that. How could she look us in the face again? Sean sits with his head in his hands, rocking backwards and forwards and moaning. I go and squeeze his shoulder but he doesn't respond.

We're all waiting to see what will happen next, when the door pushes open and there's Alice, cool as the proverbial cucumber, waving and smiling like Saturday never happened.

This is getting surreal. I'm losing the plot, wondering if I'm on some kind of hallucinogen.

Then it gets weirder. Decima tries to fire Alice, and timid little Alice basically tells her to get lost and actually winks at us. As Decima stalks away, Alice starts laughing, and says: 'Gentlemen, there may be trouble ahead…'

Cory grabs her hands and swings her around and sings: 'Let's face the music and dance.'

We're singing along with them, dancing around like little kids. The tension is broken and we're back to normality. OK, nothing is ever normal here. It's totally wacky.

Sean is doing some kind of Indian war dance, whooping and hollering. He pulls Alice into his arms, nearly knocking her over, and they stand there, locked together. It looks as if he's won. Fair play to him. I reckon they're made for each other.

Everything's turning out good. The new show is a fresh beginning for all of us, our fears are over and we're on a high.

Then I turn around, and where the door is slightly open I see Decima standing by the elevator, watching, her face twisted with fury.

A shiver runs down my back. I have a real bad feeling. It's not over at all. It's just beginning.

Dear Reader,

I hope you have enjoyed your time with Alice, Decima and the boys. This is the first novel I've ever written and it has been quite an experience. No need to try to imagine what everybody will do next – they decide and do it themselves, frequently waking me up during the night and interrupting at sometimes inconvenient moments to nudge me to write down their thoughts and deeds. I've come to love each of them, despite their faults .

This trilogy is complete, but I'm looking forward to finding out what the future holds for them all as their stories continue. If you would like to know too, do sign up to my mailing list (*http://eepurl.com/GKLiL*) and I'll keep you posted.

New authors and books rely so much on positive feedback, so if you have the time and the willingness, please do an Alice and cast a #review spell for me onto Amazon:)

May whatever you read always bring you joy,

Kelly

Twitter @KAlleynWriter
TikTok @kellyalleyn
Facebook Kelly Alleyn Page: bit.ly/443sLRm

BOOK 2
The Witch's Tale
Preview

1

Moving on

Alice

When I'm old and look back at the night of Decima's party, I'll recognize it was when I finally grew up and learned to be myself. Admittedly it was rather late in the day, after all I was almost 26, but still. Up to then I'd more or less cruised through life, keeping a low profile. I've thought a lot about why, and realize that it came down to my upbringing. This is absolutely NO criticism of my parents. I love them both dearly. My mother spent so much time with her Mottled Screecher breeding program as well as making and marketing the *Salvheal* oil, while my father Patrick has never quite understood how to deal with me and the magic powers I inherited from my mother. He was always worried I'd do something to attract unwanted attention to the family. He was never unkind, but he tended not to pay me much attention. I sort of had to bring myself up and try not to be noticed, so I've always lacked self-confidence.

That all changed that night at Decima's, and a different me stares back from the mirror now. The 'guerilla' look that didn't suit me has gone. My curves are back. I hold my chin higher, and my gaze is direct, no longer bashful. I am never again going to be pushed into doing something that doesn't feel right. Nobody should do that. I'm not embarrassed by my magical powers anymore but appreciate what a blessing they are. I'm going to start using them more. I haven't quite decided how, but I'll find a way.

I think that standing up to Decima made her respect me. It definitely gave her something to think about. She keeps calling me 'the amazing disappearing woman' and she's been grilling the guys about the 'secret'. It's no good asking them because they're as mystified as she is.

'Come on,' she said to me the other day, 'tell me how you did it.'

I smiled enigmatically and wiggled my eyebrows.

Ramon told me they've all agreed I must have put a drug in their drinks because there's no other explanation. I just winked.

Now I'm back up in my old office across the passage from Decima, no longer stuck in the tiny basement cubicle like a broken piece of furniture. I don't see so much of the boys except when Decima summons them. She's not meant to 'entertain' them up here anymore, the feng shui woman has banned it, but I still see them going by every day, often several times.

The studio is having a makeover, Decima has a completely new image and there's a deluge of sponsorship offers. She's buzzing with excitement about the new show. My phone pings all day long with messages from her.

She's upbeat, cheerful and fun to be around and she's promised that I'm going to have a bigger role in future.

It's funny how you can do something if you really have to. Because I panic being in confined spaces I've always avoided the elevator. Before, I could use **Broomstick** without anybody noticing, but now I have to go up and down to the top floor everyday, I've had to deal with it. People would start asking questions if I was never seen in it. The thought kept me awake all night before my first day up at the top. Then I reminded myself of that mad morning with Scorpio, and how I didn't give a second thought when I got in the elevator with him, so I knew I could do it. And it's glass, and rides up the outside of the Tower, so I can see out. If it should ever break down people will be able to see I'm trapped in it and they'll send help. The first day I gave myself a calming spell, but now I'm used to it. I enjoy looking over the town below as I glide up and down.

I've moved out of my old apartment. I wanted somewhere away from town, where I can enjoy fresh air to give Zylch space to play outside. I mentioned to Sean that I was looking for a change of scene. One of his musician friend's folks own a smallholding where they grow fruit, with a little converted barn which they are renting to me. It's fenced off for privacy, perfect really. Zylch can enjoy himself without any risk of being seen. I talked to him about the possibility of people turning up unexpectedly and said he'll need to transform into a cat while they're here. He stared back at me for a moment, then winked, so I'm hoping he'll behave.

My parents brought over a load of furniture from their house and helped me arrange it. Sean insisted on helping too, and we made it all feel very homely and comfortable. It's quite a way out of town, and twice as far to the Tower, but closer to the Brent Flats and very secluded. If I need it there's a bus service that passes by a short distance away, but I've started to enjoy jogging, and I can always use **Broomstick** if I feel like it.

Life's pretty good. I'm in a happy place.

Leaving the apartment for the last time I did feel a pang of sadness, remembering Jai standing there waiting for me that first time we met. I keep thinking the hole in my heart is mending, but every so often I'm hit with a stab of loss and longing. I push it away because it's in the past, and I must keep moving forwards.

Sean has been great. Every couple of days he comes to see if I need any help. He's fixed some shelving and a window that was sticking. He brought a couple of pizzas with him so we could share a meal when he'd finished. He says if I ever get lonely give him a call and he'll come over. I'm beginning to think of him as the brother I never had. I will never forget how he was ready to defend me that night at Decima's party.

2

The pond

Alice

In one of my mother's gardening magazines there's an article about ponds that really took my fancy. I asked my landlord if I could put one in, and he said to go ahead.

When I mention it to Sean, the next thing I know he's organized for the boys to come next Saturday to create it. I admit I hadn't thought through how I was going to excavate a big enough hole to start with.

'It'll take you forever,' Sean says, 'if you try to do it yourself. The guys would all be happy to help.'

We arrange that I'll order the materials and they'll all come over at the weekend to do the work, and we'll have a BBQ in the evening.

I invite my parents, my friend Shelley with her two little girls, and Decima, who looks so tired these days, with all the preparations for the new channel. I thought it would be nice for her to have some time to relax and chill.

At first she declines, saying she has another

engagement, but when I tell her that all the boys will be there too her eyes nearly pop out of her head, and she says she'll stop by for a while if she can.

I'm anxious as I've never entertained a crowd before. In fact, the nearest I've ever got to 'entertaining' was inviting Shelley for pizza, but Sean says he'll take care of the BBQ, my mother is bringing potato salad and apple pie, as well as some plants for the new pond. Shelley's going to hang lights in the trees and I don't have to do anything except make sure there's plenty of food and drink. Sean has talked Cory into being 'barman', using his butlering skills. Actually I'm not sure what a butler does, but Sean says Cory will nail it.

Sean's friend James, who lives half a mile away, surprises me, arriving with a mechanical digger that will make the job much easier. They start work in the early morning before it's too hot, and working together and with the help of the digger, it's amazing how fast the pond takes shape. I keep everybody refreshed with cold drinks. As it gets warmer the boys strip off down to their shorts. Physically they are so different. Josh's tanned chest is wide and muscled, covered with curly white hair. Cory ties his long black hair into a man bun. He and Sean are both pale-skinned and with almost hairless chests, and I can see their ribs. I make Sean put his T-shirt back on because redheads burn up so badly. I can hardly take my eyes off Ramon's body. His glossy caramel-colored skin is so smooth and unblemished as if it's been polished, and the muscles glide beneath it with a life of their own. I don't fancy him in that way, but he's an absolute work of art to look at.

They're all horsing around as they work, quite different from their behavior at the studio. You can tell they genuinely like each other.

By early afternoon the liner is in the pond and it's ready to be filled. I run the hose into it while they use the digger to spread the surplus soil around and flatten it out.

While the pool fills they go home to shower and change, except for Sean who says he needs to stay to set up the BBQ, so he showers in my bathroom and then gets busy in the kitchen, singing and whistling. That's what I like about having him around, he's always happy.

For the rest of my life I'll remember this perfect night. My mother and Sean bond over the cooking. Shelley's kids splash in the pond, and as the evening goes on and the guys have a few beers they join in. My father, who doesn't usually drink more than a beer a night, has quite a few and ends up chasing around with the hose and spraying us all. Cory and Ramon flirt with Shelley and play with the little girls. I notice James, Sean's friend who dug out the pond, watching us from the back of the garden. He's achingly shy and tongue-tied, but I persuade him to join us. Josh is sitting with him. When darkness comes Sean and Cory take up their guitars. My normally shy father, who is by now tipsier than I'd ever seen him, has them playing his favorite country and westerns, and surprises us all with his beautiful voice, even if he misses a few of the words. We join in, singing lazily, softly.

As the evening wears on we fall quieter and sit around beneath the stars, listening to the sounds of the night. I have never known such a feeling of being surrounded by friends and family. My parents lean against each other, and I go and sit close to them. From the corner of my eye I spot Zylch mischievously threading his way around us, but nobody seems to notice. Except for my mother – who winks at me. Yes, I'll never forget this night, when I'm surrounded by all those people who care for me.

Decima turns up, quite late, and brings me a beautifully wrapped plant as a housewarming gift. Wearing pencil-heeled sandals, and a skimpy, floral print dress that is almost transparent, with a matching chiffon scarf around her neck, she realizes immediately that she is out of place, and she stands around looking aloof and awkward until my mother goes into the house and brings a couple of chairs from the kitchen. She plants them next to my father, leads Decima to one, and sits down next to her chatting. Apart from waving and shouting out a greeting, none of the boys pay Decima much attention. Still, she seems to be enjoying the company of my parents, occasionally smiling and nodding her head. My father brings her a beer and they clink bottles. She doesn't stay long. Before she goes she gives my mother and father a quick hug and says she has somewhere else to be. When she leaves, I'm almost certain she has tears in her eyes;

probably from the smoke from the barbecue.

It's after midnight by the time everybody starts to leave. Sean says he's happy to stay and clear up, but Shelley is staying over with her two little girls so there's nowhere for him to sleep. He's going to come back tomorrow. My mother says she'll be here in the morning to take Shelley and the girls home.

When we're alone, Shelley says: 'I see you've made a conquest.'

'What?'

'Sean. He's crazy about you.'

'Sean? He's a good friend, that's all. So helpful, and great company. We laugh a lot.'

'Alice, are you blind? He's infatuated. You must be able to see that. He never takes his eyes off you.'

She's absentmindedly stroking Zylch, who's curled up on her lap.

I stare at her. 'Are you sure? I've never thought of him in that way – more like a brother.'

Shelley shakes her head. 'Then there's something wrong with you. Anybody can see it. And you know, he's a really nice guy, he'd be good for you.'

'I don't want anybody. I'm happy on my own.'

'That's so dumb. You don't want to spend the rest of your life alone. And there's a genuinely decent man who could make you happy if you give him a chance. Think about it, Alice. You obviously like him, and given time you may grow to love him as much as he loves you.'

After I've gone to bed, I lie awake thinking about what she said. If I'm really honest, I do realize that Sean wants to be more than just a friend, but I try to ignore it. I like his company, I value his friendship, but I'm sure I'll never love him the way he wants to be loved.

And then there's the thing with Decima. But that could be good; that part of his life would be separate, so it could work. Although I really like him as a person, in fact love him as a friend, I am not ready for a physical relationship.

He'd never be able to hurt me, and I know he never would, but there's always the risk that I could hurt him. But why would I? I will never find anybody who could replace Jai, so I'd never leave Sean for someone else and I'd never be unfaithful to him.

Maybe Shelley is right. I can't lock myself away from life, and I'm lucky that somebody as sweet as Sean cares about me.

Thoughts swirl around in my head, keeping me awake until dawn, until at last I fall asleep.

Continue reading
The BEWITCHED Trilogy

2: The Witch's Tale
Dark forces align against Alice and her tormentor
Away from the studio, there are momentous changes in Alice's personal life
whilst Decima finds the true meaning of love in an unlikely place. As their
silent skirmish continues, dark forces capable of destroying them both
align. When the world as they know it crumbles around them, an evening
of terror leads to a dramatic twist of fate.

3: Twists of Fate
A bombshell confession reveals the Tower's final secret
Through the highs and lows of love and loss, hope and fear, it takes a touch
of magic to bring Alice and Decima the true happiness they seek. In a
shocking final twist, the Tower's biggest secret is unveiled.

Available online and to order from all good bookshops worldwide.

Acknowledgements

Special thanks to Vinod Chauhan, Carole Morrow, Nelle Pettit Smith, Tanya Bullock, Jacqui Hazell, Christina Hamilton and Pam Billinge.

www.ingramcontent.com/pod-product-compliance
Lightning Source LLC
Chambersburg PA
CBHW031257120726
47906CB00003B/789